The blowholers

THE BLOWHOLERS

Books by John Reese

SURE SHOT SHAPIRO

THE LOOTERS

SUNBLIND RANGE

PITY US ALL

SINGALEE

HORSES, HONOR AND WOMEN

JESUS ON HORSEBACK: The Mooney County Saga

- ANGEL RANGE
- THE BLOWHOLERS
- THE LAND BARON

BIG HITCH

SPRINGFIELD .45-70

WEAPON HEAVY

THEY DON'T SHOOT COWARDS

ANGEL RANGE

JOHN REESE

THE BLOWHOLERS

THE BLOWHOLERS *first appeared as part of the trilogy* JESUS ON HORSEBACK: The Mooney County Saga

DOUBLEDAY & COMPANY, INC.
GARDEN CITY, NEW YORK
1974

All of the characters in this book are purely fictional, and any resemblance to actual persons, living or dead, is coincidental.

Library of Congress Cataloging in Publication Data

Reese, John Henry.
The blowholers.

"The blowholers first appeared as . . . [book 2] of the trilogy: Jesus on horseback."
I. Title.
PZ3.R25673B1 [PS3568.E43] 813'.5'4
ISBN: 0-385-03428-8
Library of Congress Catalog Card Number: 72-181793

For

ERMA McCUTCHEON CARSON

Who Knows Better . . .

THE BLOWHOLERS

CHAPTER 1

It was fixing to blizzard, a Ground Hog Day storm out'n the Rockies, with sixteen inches of January snow still on the ground, and the sleet rattling off the cabin like birdshot, and the wind whooping in the eaves. It was a good time to get a winter shave, about five of an evening, but dark as midnight. I was in my kitchen with a lantern and a lamp, stropping my razor while my whiskers soaked, with the tops of my underwear hanging down around my belt. I'll never forget.

I thought I heard Ownie Cope complaining to me, so I said, "What? What you bellyaching about now?"

Ownie was a worthless kind of a kid who was holed up with me until I could think of a way to get rid of him. He didn't answer, and when I looked into the common room, he was still laying asleep on a bench, nine points drunk.

I heard it again then, and knowed it was this new dog of mine, that an Indian left with me for security, when he stole a bridle. If you're going to do business with tame Indians, you've got to do it their way, and this was my dog until the Indian wore out the bridle and brought it back. Its mother was half wolf, and its Indian name sounded like V.G., so I called it V.G.

My other dogs, Spot and Foolish, began to bark. I pulled up my underwear and put on my coat and earflap cap, and went out with my lantern. Spot and Foolish was in the root cellar, and V.G. was on a chain where he could get into the barn, only he never did, and liked to sleep outside in the worst weather.

Spot was the mother of Foolish, and a good watchdog. They had heard the noise too, and had come up the steps and was looking out through a crack in the door of the root cellar. Her and me looked at each other like we both wanted to know what was wrong, so they had just been barking because V.G. had barked.

I went over to V.G. and saw him leaning against his chain, trying to smell downwind, and not even a wolf can do that. Most people needed a club in their hand whenever they got close to V.G., but I never had no trouble with him.

"What's the matter there, dog?" I asked him.

He made that kind of a whiny, howly noise that went for a bark with him, and I knowed something was down there. I hollered, "Is somebody out there? Who's there? What do you want?"

Not a sound answered, and I wished I'd had sense enough to put on my gun, and when I get that feeling, usually it's right. A man can't always pick and choose who his visitors are going to be, especially somebody like me.

I had this place near the homestead country in northeast Colorado, Pete Heath's Place, where I ran a poker game, and sold groceries, and a little whisky, and could fix you a meal if you was content with stew or good plain fried cooking. A few pilgrims stopped there, that didn't dare show up nowhere else. They knowed me and I knowed them from old times, and there was a rule that nobody ever made trouble for me, because then they wouldn't have no place where people in a hurry could fill their bellies and rest their horses.

I had been on the wrong side of the law in my time, I admit that freely, and Pete Heath is not my family name, but after I got a few wounds in me I had swore off the outlaw game, and everybody knowed it. I was prob'ly the safest man in Colorado without a gun, as a general rule.

But the only general rule about people I believe in is that you never can tell. I started to blow out the lantern, but I changed my mind, because if somebody is about to ambush you, this is just daring him to take his shot while he can. I headed back toward the house with it, and here came Ownie Cope, blundering around in the dark.

"Why didn't you leave a light on?" he said. "Who was you hollering at out there?"

The lamp in the kitchen had blowed out when I went outside, and Ownie had banged himself on the side of the head on a shelf, and he wasn't either drunk or sober to begin with, but just mean. "I don't know if it's anybody," I said, "but I'll get my gun and find out."

"I'll go with you," he said.

"You'll go back inside is what you'll do," I said.

"You don't give me no orders," he said.

"This time I do," I said. "I don't want to hunt down some fool sot that fell down and half froze to death."

"Did you call me a fool sot?" he said.

"Yes I did," I said.

Ownie was maybe twenty-two, a big tall lean skinny big-boned kid that had been around a lot. Born of a woman that rode the Mississippi steamboats, he said, and she died when he was about ten. He lived with her relations in St. Louis, but they kept dinging him about his mother being a loose woman, and they fed him sparingly and whipped him generously. So he went over the fence when he was thirteen, and it seemed to me he had never stopped running.

Ownie was a cowboy by trade, a real nothing job, and he fancied himself a hellion with cards and a gun. He was a good poker player until he started to win, and then you could see through him like he had a glass head. He played a good hand when he was losing, but you ain't going to make no money playing good losing poker.

Ownie was always practicing the fast draw, and he loved to talk about the gunfighters that had left their name and fame wherever people take it serious. He had never killed nobody, but he was a cinch to do it someday if I was any judge, which I was. Or get killed himself.

Ownie had the big hands a gunman needs, and you couldn't fault him for nerve, but a good gunfighter ain't fighting the bottle if I'm any judge, and I was. Ownie had long yella hair and blue eyes, and a kind of a pitiful look like a lost dog, until you got him mad. When Ownie Cope got mad, he had the meanest blue eyes you ever seen.

He got mad now, and said nobody was going to call him a fool sot, and took hold of my arm. I give him a good shake and got rid of him, and went back to the house and got my holster down off'n its nail. Ownie blundered along after me.

"You son of a bitch, what do you mean, calling me a name like that, Pete?" he said. "I thought we was friends."

I pulled the gun out and stuck it in his belly, and thumbed the hammer back slow, so he could hear both the safety click and the full-cock click. "Only my true friends can make free with that name, boy," I said, "and nobody's a true friend who makes things worse when they're already bad enough. Cover the lamp when I go out."

I lit the lamp and went out and left him grumbling. Oh but it was dark! I couldn't hear a sound except V.G. whining, but I had this strange odd feeling I wasn't alone. Spot and Foolish had went back down where it was warm, where there was a weighted door to let them in and out without freezing my potatoes and onions and turnips. But V.G. was still leaning on a tight chain, and when he seen me coming, he whined and wagged his tail.

I unsnapped his chain from the steeple in the barn wall and said, "Let's go then, V.G." He took off down the wind, pulling like a colt, me blundering along behind on the other end of the chain.

It had started to snow, hard and fast, and my lantern just wasn't no use at all. I had a kind of a winding, twisting road from the Mooney wagon road to my place, because when I chopped the brush out for it, I was looking for easy brush to chop, ruther than a straight road. Right down that winding road through them light trashy trees we went.

V.G. stopped suddenly, and here was a man on his face in the middle of my road. "Damn it, somebody has got himself shot on my doorstep practically," I said to myself, "and I'll have that sheriff over me like a swarm of bees, what a Ground Hog Day this has been."

You'd expect a quarter-strain wolf dog just to tear a man's throat open that was laying helpless like that, but V.G. didn't. I put the lantern down where it wouldn't tip over, and holstered my gun, and got down on my knees as fast as I could, considering my old wounds.

I turned him over and seen he was no more than a boy, with his whole front one big slab of frozen blood. I never seen nobody lose that much blood and live, but he was still warm to touch, and he had got this far. It was up to me. I couldn't get a sound out of him, and he didn't so much as twitch, but when a person is still warm, you've got to figure he still has a chance.

I've got no business packing a load, the shape I'm in, but there's times when you've got no choice. I eased this boy up without straining myself, and hefted him over my shoulders. I picked up my lantern and started back toward the cabin, feeling my way through the snow.

Somehow I lost V.G.'s chain, and he streaked off into the storm, and I didn't know whether to curse him or me. I just kept hobbling along, one grunt at a time, with them old bullet holes pulling at me. If I'd of cut that road straight, I'd of been all right. But I only got around one hairpin turn, when I knowed I wasn't going to make it all the way, not with this kid on my shoulder.

Just then here come Ownie hanging on the end of the chain, with V.G. on the other end, dragging him along. Ownie could always get along with a horse or a dog, and once he even tamed a chipmunk to come to him, and once a blue jay, and he never had showed no fear of V.G. But I didn't expect nobody to catch that dog once he got loose.

"How did you catch him?" I said.

"Catch him? Hell, he like to tore the door down, trying to catch *me,*" Ownie said. "What have you got here? Let me have him, before you tear your fool guts out. Why, he ain't no bigger than a pound of hen feathers!"

He took the kid over his arms like a baby. Ownie could sober up fast when he had to, and he surely had sobered up when V.G. started fighting that door. Now you tell me why a dog would do a thing like that, for human beans that kept him on a chain, and hardly had a kind word for him! But that's what that dog had done, he went back there and got Ownie to help me.

I packed the lantern, and Ownie packed the kid, and we got to the cabin. When I opened the door, V.G. shot in ahead of me, the first time he had ever been in a human house that I knowed of, and went straight to the bedroom. Now you tell me how he knowed where it was!

The lamp blowed out again, but I still had the lantern. While Ownie was putting the boy down on the bed, I got a big two-burner coal-oil lamp from the common room, and brought it to the bedroom, and lit both wicks.

"Why he's just a kid!" Ownie said. "What a hell of an age to get all cut up or shot, whichever it was."

"Let's peel him down and dress his wounds," I said. "You got to figure he's got a chance, if he's still warm."

All the kid had on was a canvas jacket, and an old cowhide vest, and farmer overhalls half wore out, and no shirt or underwear. He had on cowboy boots without socks, but he sure didn't look like no cowboy, and the dirtiest feet you ever seen. He had long black tangly hair, like an Indian, and a few black whiskers, but if he had ever shaved in his life, it was just showing off.

But there wasn't a wound on him anywhere! Nothing but two big juicy welts across his back, where somebody had whipped him, and a few bruises here and there.

"He's stove up bad inside, to bleed so from his mouth," Ownie said. "He's as good as dead. God damn anybody that would beat a kid like that!"

I told Ownie to set with him while I got him something warm to eat. I'd made a nice big stew earlier in the week, beef and cottontail rabbit and venison, and two teal and a canvasback, with potatoes and onions and turnips and carrots and okra and some Mexican chilis I'd been able to raise in my rocky old garden. I kept it froze in a big kettle in the lean-to off the kitchen.

I chopped off a chunk with the hatchet, and put it in a pot on the kitchen stove, and throwed some pine knots into the fire. I got it thawed out fast, but then I couldn't get more than a little dribble of the gravy down this kid.

"His guts is ruined," Ownie said. "The poor little pitiful son of a bitch, to die so young!"

"Let's try the sovereign remedy," I said, handing him the key to the chest. "The store whisky."

"The creek shine is better," Ownie said. "You know, Pete, this is the first time you ever let me have the key to the whisky chest."

"And the last time, and make it store whisky," I said. "Them nesters out on the creek make shine out of anything, even boiled corncobs. Just pour a little in the cup and lock the chest."

"Don't take any myself, you mean," he said. "You sure are a friendly sociable bastard sometimes."

He brought me the cup and my key, and I poured a little of the tanglefoot into the kid's mouth, and like to strangled him. I had Ownie put a little water in it, and some sugar, and tried it again.

The thing about whisky, it'll bring the spit when food won't, and an unconscious man will swallow it when he won't swallow anything else, because of the flow of spit. The kid kind of wiggled and moaned, and I started slopping it to him, a sip of whisky and water, and then a spoon of the stew.

I got almost a cup of the stew down him before he just kind of slid off asleep. "If his guts is ruined," I said, "he'll die anyway, and if they ain't, and he's just asleep, maybe he'll live."

"He's got some red in his face now," Ownie said. "He looks better to me. If he don't make it, he'll at least die drunk, that's some consolation."

"He's a dirty little varmint," I said. "I sure hope he don't bug up my bed."

"Lice or bedbugs would starve on what's left of his blood," Ownie said. "I sure would like to know who done that to him. I'd take a blacksnake whip to him, and when I had cut him up a little, I'd put a .45 in his mouth and pull the trigger with a clean conscience."

I told him he made my hind end tired with that kind of bloodthirsty talk. We put a blanket over the kid, and left the bedroom door open so the fireplace in the common room could warm it up in there, and went back to the kitchen. I finished shaving. Every now and then, Ownie would take a candle and tiptoe in and look at this dirty little naked kid on my bed.

"He ain't so pale, and he seems to be just nice and sound asleep," he said each time. Then finely he set down and said, "Pete, that kid is going to make it! I'll make you a little bet, four bits against two, he lives."

I was getting pretty tired of him. I said, "What do you care? What's it to you, Ownie, if he lives or dies?"

"What's it to me?" he said. "That's a hell of a thing to say!"

"Why is it?" I said. "When did you ever think of anybody but yourself before in your whole life? Now here you are, slobbering like a missionary with pity. Do you mean old worthless Ownie Cope has turned over a new leaf?"

He had to think that over. "Maybe I been waiting for somebody in a worse fix than me, and finely I've found him," he said.

"I don't know what you've got to complain about," I said. "Ownie, life is what you make it."

"The hell it is," he said. "Tell that to that kid in there, if he lives long enough to listen. A fine chance he's got to make a life, at his age!"

"How about at your age?" I said.

He asked what I meant by that, and I told him he was old enough to know better and young enough to change his ways, and still was one of the most worthless people I knowed. I told him the mother that bore him might as well of dropped him on a rock, and saved the world the trouble. He said the mother that bore him was only a steamboat whore, and I said I was tired of listening to him complain about her, and he said if I wasn't already so stove up, he'd pound them words back into me. I said to go ahead and try.

Thus we passed the night, not what you'd call sociable, but at least interesting.

CHAPTER 2

Late in the night, the kid began clawing at his hair and screaming about snakes, and we couldn't quiet him down and we couldn't wake him up. We just had to hold onto him until suddenly he quit fighting and dozed off again. We went back into the kitchen.

"He don't act like somebody all busted up inside," I said.

"It's that store whisky, Pete," Ownie said. "He's got the delirious trembles, that's all."

But he agreed with me, the kid wasn't as bad hurt as he looked. A while later, we heard him moan, and when we went in with a lantern, he was wide awake. I had the stew in a pot on the back of the stove, so I left Ownie with him while I fetched it. He let me spoon a little of it to him, and then he grabbed the spoon and wolfed it down himself.

"That's all they is?" he said, when it was gone.

"There's plenty more, but you better take it easy," I told him. "A little at a time, that's the ticket."

He didn't thank me, just laid down and looked around liked a trapped coyote, trying to figure out where he was, and who Ownie and me was, and how he'd got there. Then his eyelids sagged, and off he went to sleep, just like that.

Hour or so later, we heard him rustling around. We went in with the lantern and caught him stumbling around in the dark, trying to be quiet. He grabbed a quilt to cover himself and said, "Whar's my clothes? Who stoled my clothes? I got to go find my sisters!"

"What's left is in the woodshed," I said. "I'll find you some clothes when you're able to go out."

"Able hell!" he said. "God dang you, git me my clothes, I want my clothes, whar's my clothes?"

He didn't talk pure hillbilly, but it was mostly that, and he didn't have no more manners than a hog. That old narrow dark face of his was just mean as a cornered skunk, and his eyes glittered through that hair of his like they'd catch it afire.

"You can't go nowhere in this storm," I said. "Get some more rest, and then eat some more if your guts is up to it. You was just covered with blood, and there ain't a mark on you except some whip marks, so likely you throwed up the blood."

"That's my pappy's blood, and from my nose," he said, and began to cry a little. "God dang you, git me my clothes so I can go look for my sisters!"

"Pete, he can eat," Ownie said. "Let's feed the little varmint some more, and see if we can tame him."

"You do it," I said. "I'll get him some clothes."

Ownie hacked off another lump of stew and het it up, and I got some clothes out of the chest. Somebody comes along now and then wanting clothes, usually so they won't answer somebody's description, and they know they can make a swap at Pete Heath's Place. I found a shirt and pants, and some drawers and an undershirt, and a blanket coat. When I come back through the kitchen with them, Ownie was filling up the stew bowl again.

"Movers!" he said. "Why didn't we let him freeze?"

"I reckoned he was a mover when I heard that hillbilly talk," I said. "Did you find out who whipped him?"

"I was too busy watching him eat. You could feed a teaming crew cheaper, I swear to goodness," Ownie said.

We took the clothes and the stew to the bedroom. The kid ate while I laid out the clothes. "Jesus, drawers! I never had drawers before," he said.

I didn't say nothing. He just set there huddled up in a blanket and pumped the stew into himself.

"I had a bad dream, didn't I last night?" he said.

"You sure did," I said.

"Once when I was little in Tennessee, I walked under a tree limb, and there was a big old copperhead wropped around it, and he dangled against my head," he said. "Every time I get sick, I dream I got that snake wropped around my neck and can't get him off."

"So you come from Tennessee," I said.

He narrowed his eyes and just shivered. "You'ns get out of here, so I can get dressed," he said.

Nobody is as particular about being seen naked as somebody so poor he can't afford under-drawers. Me and Ownie went back to the kitchen and closed the door.

"Movers, by God!" Ownie said. "Stomp on them before they can multiply, I always say. Movers!"

Movers is the most hopeless people on earth. They say they're going to the gold fields, or Oregon, or the Sacramento Valley, or the Qu' Appelle Basin, someplace where a poor man has got a chance. But they ain't going nowhere, they're going *from*, not to. They couldn't settle down and amount to anything where they was, and they ain't going to settle down and amount to anything anywhere else, either.

They're mostly hillbillies, the men poison mean, always packing pistols and knives, and a rifle in easy reach, and the women usually just dirty sluts. The old ones is ugly and toothless and always chewing snuff, and the young ones is usually trying to get you off into the brush, only if you get caught at it, you're as good as dead or gelded. Sometimes you can hand the man a five-dollar gold piece, and he'll forget it unless it's his own wife. If it's his sister or daughter, he'll whine he ought to have more, in case she gets your child, and she was a pure girl until you tolled her off into the brush. Who prob'ly tolled her off the first time was her uncle or cousin, because movers is like pigs out of the same litter, they don't care who they breed to.

They have some old sore-backed horses to pull a covered wagon with, and a couple they can't drive, because they're something wrong with them and all they're good for is to trade. You trade a mover out of a decent horse, you can be sure he stole him.

They'll trade harness too, or pigs or dogs or pots and pans, and while your back is turned they'll steal you blind. If you run them off your place, they'll come back at night and burn you out, or kill your own pigs or sheep and throw them down your own well.

They live their whole lives in them wagons, going from New-Brasky to the gold fields or Oregon or someplace, and they hate everybody that's settled down, and you offer one a few days' work, he's insulted. They live on game, rabbits and squirrels and ground hogs and the like, or somebody's chickens or shotes, and all it takes besides that is a little corn meal and salt.

The kid come slinking out of the bedroom in his new clothes. "Howdy," he said. "I'd like to borry a horse now, please, to go find my sisters."

A mover that will say "please" is the albino in the litter for sure. I thought maybe this kid could be tamed after all. I said, "Look at how it's storming, kid. You wouldn't get a hundred feet in this weather."

"You try to holt me!" he said.

"I won't hold you," I said, "but leave your clothes behind, because they won't be no good if I have to break them off'n your corpse when this storm lets up."

He made a jump and grabbed a meat cleaver off the wall, and come at me screaming, "Give me my own clothes then, God durn your soul, or I'll cut your heart out!"

I retch behind me for the broom, but Ownie said, "Pete, leave this cub catamount to me. He reminds me too much of my own self at the same age, only he's dirtier."

I went into the common room and waited there. I heard Ownie and the kid talking in the kitchen, and then the kid went into the bedroom and slammed the door, and then Ownie went in after him. They was in there at least half an hour, and then the door opened and Ownie come out and closed it behind him. He set down in a chair in the kitchen and began cursing, just God-damning everything, starting with the day the world was created and working up to the present time, going at it slow so he wouldn't miss anything.

I went into the kitchen. "Where is he?" I said.

"Asleep," Ownie said. "Pete, there's a kid who had even less chance in life than me."

"I hope he makes more of what little he's got," I said. "Did you find out anything about him?"

"I found out everything," Ownie said, "and it would just make you crazy mad at the world, when things like this can happen to people."

The kid's father was named John Houten Swiverton, only the kid called him his pap, not father, and said Pap was dead now. The kid's name was Houten Saul Swiverton, and he went by the name of Hoot. He was fifteen, and his sister Alice was fourteen, and his sister Liddie was seventeen. Their mother was dead a long time ago.

They come from Lapland, down in the Ozarks, where Arkansas laps over into Missouri, and before that Tennessee, and before that Kentucky, only the kid couldn't remember that. The mother had died in McDonald County, Missouri, and Pap was on his way to file on land in Wyoming, where a poor man had a chance.

"And by the Eternal, Pete, this one I believe!" Ownie said. "This wasn't no ordinary mover trash."

In Nebraska last summer, one of their horses give out and died, and Pap had to work in the hayfields to earn another one. Then Pap gave out too. Hoot and the girls between them made a haying hand enough to buy a horse, and two weaned heifer calves, and they lit out for Wyoming again. The old pap swore to get them kids out of the wagons if it was the last act of his life.

"He almost made it, too," Ownie said, "and it sure wasn't his fault he didn't. God damn such a world as this one! Where is your law when things like this can go on?"

They had come through here week before last, missing the towns and the main roads, keeping to their own selves all they could. The horses was getting tired and they knowed a storm couldn't help but hit soon, and if they was going to be snowed in for the winter, they wanted to pick the place.

A couple of days ago, they found a nice flat canyon full of bluestem that hadn't all been snowed under, to the north and west of my place some eight or ten miles. I thought I knowed the canyon they meant. Anyway they made a camp there, and butchered one of the calves. They hated to kill a calf that would make them a milker in Wyoming, but they had no choice, they hadn't seen a deer or antelope in weeks, and the old pap didn't have no ammunition left for his guns even if they had.

They staked the team out, and hung up tarps so Hoot and Pap could sleep under the wagon, while Alice and Liddie slept in it. They killed the calf and cooked the liver the first night, and cut the rest of it up to smoke over their fire.

Yesterday morning they was just going to go out and get more firewood, when they looked up and seen four riders on a ridge about half a mile away. They didn't do nothing, just set there watching, and the old pap began to get worried. He told Hoot he wished they'd been harnessed up, but there wasn't no use trying to move out now. That would just dare them four to come down and devil them.

He had the girls get in the wagon and stay there, and he made sure he had his knife handy. The girls got in the wagon, but it was too late for that. Them four riders come jogging their horses down slow, like they didn't know what they wanted. But the old pap did.

"Hoot," he said, "you take my slatto, and I'll take the meat knife, and you promise me this: If they kill me, you kill your sisters before you let anybody have them."

A slatto was what the hillbillies called a long thin stabbing knife, a stiletto. Hoot said, "Oh God, Pap, you cain't mean that, I got to kill Alice and Liddie!"

"You'll be sorry if you don't," Pap said.

They was four of the raunchiest, dirtiest, worst-looking roughnecks he'd ever seen, Hoot said, only to save his soul he couldn't tell now what a single one of them looked like. What happened was just so horrible his mind had went blank, and he only remembered what his old pap had said because Pap was right, he was sorry he hadn't got a chance to kill his sisters.

He remembered seeing one of them chasing Liddie on his horse, and he remembered Alice fighting with two of them inside the wagon, and his pap going at them with a knife. He didn't remember the shooting, but he did remember his pap laying there on his back in the snow, his chest and belly just shot to pieces. That's how he got all that blood on himself, when he throwed himself down on his pap and blubbered, "Oh no, Pap, you can't be dead yet, Pap, oh my God, Pap, git up and help me help the girls."

He remembered one of them four men on his horse laughing, and he went at him with the slatto, but the man hit him over the back with his quirt and just kept hitting him until he could catch him over the eye with the heel of his boot. Out he went.

When he come to, they was trying to burn the wagon, only it wouldn't burn. They throwed the calf meat down so the coyotes could get it, and just rode out of there. And Hoot couldn't describe a single one of them! It had just went out of his mind, how they looked.

He didn't have no idee where his sisters was, and when he hollered for them, nobody answered. He started to foller the tracks of the four horses. He follered them all day, but when night came, he was in amongst some trashy softwood trees. He knowed he couldn't foller nothing through the dark amongst them trees.

He pulled some dry grass out from under the snow, and got out his flint and steel and made a little fire. He aimed to night there, and start again in the morning; only then it started to blizzard, and he knowed that by morning, the tracks would all be gone.

He broke off a couple of limbs and made himself torches, and he follered the tracks through the dark to a little winding road. He come to a place where them four had stood their horses quite a while, before they rode off in another direction, almost due west, at a gallop.

Hoot knowed he was at least a day behind them, and afoot in a storm. He just wanted to set down and cry, only that wouldn't do no good. About then, he thought he seen a light through the trees and brush. He started towards it, and that was the last thing he knowed before he woke up in my bed.

"Them four was from the blowhole," Ownie said.

"Like as not," I said.

"And I tell you something else, they was heading here for your place, Pete," he said.

"Ownie," I said, "I been in trouble in my time, and I get some curious people in here, yes I do. But I run a legal wayside inn, and the sheriff trusts me, and he's got a perfect right to. Nobody from the blowhole feels free to stop in here, and so let's not have any of that kind of loose talk starting around."

Ownie was headachy from the drinking, and nervous as a spring bear. He drummed on the table with his fingers a minute like he hadn't heard me. He said, "I didn't mean they figured they could hole up here," he said. "You'd of got the same thing old pap got. They meant to hole up here, and you know what scared them off? Me!"

"I just bet," I said. "A man with your virtuous reputation, why it would just scare them to death!"

He kept drumming with his fingers. "Have all the fun you like," he said, "but by God, Pete, one of them murdering bastards knows about me. He seen my horse in the stable is why they changed their minds about raiding this place. Four of that kind, why they're only about six men short of making it an even fight against me, and they damn well knowed it!"

He set there cursing, calling them every filthy name he could think of, and he had a mind that run to that kind of words. But he wasn't fooling me. I knowed that what made him so all-fired bitter was that, in his heart, he knowed he wasn't a whole lot better than they was.

He hadn't fell that low, not yet anyway. But give him time, he was headed for the blowhole sure.

Northwest by west of my place about fifteen miles was this big hillside that you could spot as far as you could see it. There was this big bald ten-acre sand hole on the side where nothing would grow, not even cactus. There was a little brush around it, but nothing in it, and this was what you call a blowhole.

In wet weather, sometimes silky sleeper-grass or milkweed thistles would start there, but they died the minute it dried out. Then the blowhole changed like the ocean, sometimes making nice even ripples, other times big rough waves. It all depended on the wind.

The color changed too. Wet, it was a kind of a dirty brown, but when it dried out, it was a light tan or sometimes kind of an orange, depending on the light. There wasn't no feed to speak of for several miles, and no water, and no reason for anybody to pass there.

That's how this riffraff got to hanging out there. There's a kind of person that seeks his own level, and he sure ain't going to find it in a prosperous cow country, or even amongst the nesters. That means work, and there's this kind of man that won't work, that only wants to drink and raise hell and rob somebody, and once you get west of the Missouri River, the country is full of them.

Men like them drift into the Badlands, or up the Gila, or into the Superstitions—any place too worthless for decent law-abiding working people. The blowholers wasn't what you'd call a gang, not by any means. They came and they went, and most of the time there wasn't nobody there. Then some cowboy tracking a lost calf would see a fire up there, and he knowed where his calf had went, and he also knowed better than to go asking questions up there.

Instead he went to the sheriff of Mooney County, Sheriff Abe Whipple. Abe rode up there when he got these complaints and kicked their camps to pieces, and burned their shanties, but generally they seen him coming and he never got so much as a look at the blowholers themselves.

That was the lonesomest place! When you get run out of a place like that, you're about as low-down as a man can get. It was no wonder Ownie Cope felt so mean. He wasn't no more than a step and a half away from the blowhole himself, and I reckon he finely faced up to it.

CHAPTER 3

The storm let up at daylight. Me and Ownie dug my wagon out of the snow and harnessed four horses, and fed them a good bait of oats. Ownie saddled up his horse. We would of left Hoot behind, because he wasn't in good shape at all yet, but we'd of had to tie him. And he had the right to go, you couldn't deny that.

There was a little blue sky when we left, and patches of fast-moving sunlight, but it was only a hole in the storm. Ownie rode ahead, breaking trail. I had all I could do with four horses on an empty wagon behind him, in places. Hoot set there on the seat beside me, trying to recognize things, but it was all strange to him.

A couple of eagles was out, cruising for something to drop on, but nothing was alive and moving closer than the homestead country, and you can bet the Kincaiders was out with guns to protect lambs or pigs or even dogs caught out in this one. By the way them eagles was tossed around, I knowed the wind was still blowing hard up there. I was in a pure frenzy to get where we was going and back, before it set in to blizzard again.

We stopped every now and then to rest the horses and eat some cold biscuits and pork sausage I'd fried up. Hoot would just nibble was all. Then we'd go on again.

We come to this stand of light cottonwoods, and Hoot set up straight and looked around. "I allow I come through these trees," he said finely.

I said, "I reckon you did, Hoot, but we got a ways to go yet, if I know where we're going. And I bet I do."

We wasn't heading for nowhere near the blowhole. We had to go around them trees on account of the wagon, and the minute we was in the clear, Hoot set up straight again and started to feel for his knife that he'd lost.

"Whoa now, boy!" I said. "That's just a tame old tramp Indian, Charley Polk. He wouldn't harm nobody."

Charley was up in his sixties and had never done a day's work in his life, and he drank too much and stole a little, but me and him always got along. Charley was over there in the foothills where the timber got heavier, waving to me. I waved back to him and told Ownie to rest the team and let me have his horse.

"A God-durned lazy Indian, well I like that!" Ownie said. "We got to stop what we're doing to see what he wants."

But he let me have his horse. I rode over to where Charley was waiting.

"What are you doing out with a four-horse team in this kind of weather, looking for a woman?" Charley said.

"Yes, a couple of them, Charley," I said.

"Only got one," Charley said. "I found her running around yesterday. This one go crazy, Pete. Crazy!"

"I'll take her off'n your hands," I said, "and then let's see if we can find the other one."

He got up behind me, and we rode to his place in the trees, half cave and half wickiup, with a nice stone fireplace, and room for him to curl up in, and not much else. He had put this girl in there last night, and he slept out in the storm. An Indian has got a lot of respect for somebody that's out of their mind, and she sure was.

She was just setting there in the dugout and staring, wilder than any squaw you ever seen, with the same black eyes and black hair that Hoot had, only her hair was down to her waist, and tangled up with twigs and grass and dirt. She was barefoot, and she had on an old brown dress and an old tore shawl.

"Which one are you?" I said to her.

She didn't answer, and Charley Polk said, "I don't think she talk, Pete. Crazy!"

I said let's try again. I got down on my knees so I could see into the dugout better, and asked her which she was, Liddie or Alice. She didn't pay me no attention, none at all, and I knowed if I went in there after her, I was going to have a wildcat on my hands, poor thing.

"I don't know what to do, Charlie," I said. "There's supposed to be two of them. We got their brother, Hoot, with us. Hoot made it as far as my place. Some of them blowholers savaged them considerable yesterday."

"Oh, them sons of bitches," Charley said.

"Hoot," the girl said. "Hoot. Hoot."

I thought I might be getting through to her, so I went on talking to Charley. I said, "Hoot is fine. He's a good boy, that Hoot. He wants to find his sisters real bad. Hoot is nice and warm and safe, and he wants Alice and Liddie to be nice and warm too. Hoot is a good brother, Hoot is."

It was like breaking through the ice. She come out of the shanty like a cork out of the jug. "I'm Liddie," she said. "You say you've got Hoot? Is Hoot all right?"

"Yes," I said, "and he's a mighty good boy."

"Not a boy," she said, and began to cry and blubber and wring her hands. "Not a boy. He fit like a man and he cursed like a man, and he'll never be a boy again, never!"

She didn't know where she was or how she'd got there, but when I told her, she tried to shake Charley Polk's hand, and when he was ashamed to do it, she grabbed it in both of hers and kissed it. Then I got up on Ownie's horse, and Charley hoisted her up behind me, and we headed back to the wagon.

She told me what she knowed, which wasn't much. She'd got away because the minute them blowholers rode up, she had sense enough to run and keep on running. One of them rode after her and tried to rope her, but he was drunk and missed her three times.

The fourth time, he got a loop over her, but she was ready for it. She catched it and jerked it off and swang the loop at the pony's face. It stood up on its hind legs and throwed this man right on his back.

What this wildcat aimed to do was steal his horse and ride off, and if that ain't pure undefiled gall, I never heard of gall. She would of made it except the horse got away. She picked up a rock instead, and hit this fella over the side of the head, and then she outrun him.

Run was all she could do, and once he caught his horse, he was going to rope her again, and this time he wasn't going to let her pull him out of no saddle. He caught his horse and finely did spot her, but she got across a little canyon with an icy crick at the bottom, and he couldn't make his horse cross.

He took a couple of shots at her with his .45, but she got away. At least she thought she did.

An hour or so later, here they come again. They must of talked it over and decided they couldn't take a chance on her getting away to live and tell on them. She got into the trees then, and dodged and hid and backtracked, and five or six times at least, she was laying there in the snow behind some brush while they set and talked it over less than a dozen feet away.

They finely give up on her, and she started walking again, until she went out of her mind. She couldn't remember Charley Polk finding her, or anything. All she knowed was that there was a fire and a soft place to sleep, and she could rest and warm her feet at last.

Her and Hoot hardly spoke to each other when we got to the wagon. Movers is a curious people. They don't like to have you looking on when it's family business, so I just let her have my seat on the wagon, and I walked ahead of the team to help break trail for them.

In another mile, their camp come in sight, just where I knowed it would be.

The most curious thing was the other girl, right out there in plain sight! She had a fire going, and the crane rebuilt, and a pot hanging from it, and water boiling so hard you could see the steam from a mile away. She seen us coming and run towards us, laughing and waving.

"Y'all's just in time, Hoot," she said. "I'm fixing a bait, just venison and dumplings is all, but I got salt too. Dumplings without salt ain't fitten."

Hoot jumped out of the wagon and grabbed her by the arm. "Where'd you get venison and stuff to make dumplings? Where'd you get salt?" he said to her.

Liddie jumped down in the snow, bare feet and all. "Let her be, Hoot, let her be!" she said.

"But God durn it, what's she talking about?" Hoot hollered. He was about to cry.

Ownie rode over to the fire, and then over to me. He said, "Pete, my God, there ain't nothing in that pot but plain water. She's crazier than the first one!"

"Maybe it's better this way," I said. "She was the one got caught here, poor little tyke."

We had an awful time trying to get her into the wagon. Them blowholers had wrecked the covered wagon, but Alice couldn't see that. No sir, as soon as they got another team, they'd go on to Wyoming and file under the Kincaid Act, and get out of the wagon the way Pap promised.

She showed us where them blowholers had shot the two horses, and she showed us her pap's body. "Sh-h-h!" she said. "Pap's sleeping late today, poor old man. Pap works so hard for us!"

Hoot just cried like a baby. Liddie wanted to cry too, but there was a girl that could save her tears when she had to. Her job was to get Alice into our wagon, and one way or another, she done it. We loaded the old pap's body in, and covered it with what was left of the wagon sheet, and I got them four tired horses turned around again, and we started back to my place.

Ownie rode back and kicked that pot of boiling water over the fire. He had to do something violent or blow up himself.

Alice set on the wagon seat with me, while Hoot and Liddie rode in the wagon box with Pap's body. I tried to talk to her about these four blowholers.

"What did they look like, honey?" I said.

She laughed and said oh, she couldn't remember what they looked like. "Only they was mean, real mean," she said, and laughed some more.

"Did you hear any of them use anybody's names?" I said.

"Oh, I didn't pay no 'tention to names," she said, and laughed. "But I scratched them. I scratched them good! They cursed something pitiful. Oh how they could curse!"

She laughed. I wasn't getting nowhere, and it was making Liddie and Hoot cry. When I left her alone, Alice just set there beside me, snuggling up to keep warm, and talking about how nice it was going to be when they got to Wyoming and could put in a garden and set some hens.

"And never have to live in no wagon no more!" she said.

"Pap said it ain't fitten to bring up girls in a wagon, and Pap keeps his promises, he does."

She wasn't like the other two so much. Liddie was kind of a tall girl, and dark like Hoot, but Alice was one of them little chubby girls, and her hair was brown instead of black, and it curled up at the ends and around her ears. It would just break your heart, she was so pretty and happy and carefree. Her mind had went completely.

I pushed them four horses worse than I like to punish a horse, but I got there before the storm got too bad. I let Ownie and Hoot take care of the team, while I went in with the girls to kick up the fire. I'd left Spot and Foolish in the root cellar, and V.G. chained to the stable, and V.G. wouldn't stand for strangers feeding him.

After I got the fire going, and Liddie to peeling potatoes, I said I had to go out and take care of my dogs. "Oh, let me go too!" Alice said. "I love dogs. We always had a dog back in Missouri."

"No, you stay and help your sister," I said.

"Oh no, let me feed the dogs," she said.

She started to run for the door. I catched her by the bare arm and held her, and when I felt the fever in her, I knowed she was a real sick girl. She was as hot as fire, and she fought me like a tiger.

Ownie come in and seen me rassling her. He let out one yell, "Alice! Stop that now! God dang you, behave yourself and stay in the God-dang house, and get into that bedroom before I have to whale the hell out of you."

Alice stopped fighting and went into the bedroom, not really scared it seemed to me, just out of habit, more. I got some meat for the dogs and went out with it, and Ownie follered me outside.

"That's how white trash talk to their kids," he said.

I said, "Ownie, it worked. That's the main thing. Don't start telling me how bad a time you had as a kid. This is one night I won't stand for it."

"I just wanted you to know why I hollered and swore at her, is all," he said. "Pete, I wouldn't talk to that girl for any other reason that way. I knowed it would work. What kind of a bastard do you think I am?"

"Just the ordinary kind," I said. "Nothing special. Your kind come in herds."

"Oh, listen to the deacon!" he said. "Let me feed the wolf, you pious son of a bitch."

I give him the meat, and dad-blamed if he didn't go over there and get down on his knees beside V.G., and feed him a piece at a time out of his hand. I couldn't even do that with V.G. myself. He'd take your hand off.

I didn't need no lantern to get around my own place. I had a nice snug barn here that would hold ten horses, and Hoot was still in there fooling around with a pitchfork, dunging out from under the horses and throwing them fresh bedding. He had a lantern hanging from a peg to see by.

I started to go in and see what was left that I could do to help finish up. Only just then, Hoot leaned his fork up against the barn wall, and put his face down against one of my horses, and wrapped his arms around his head, and began to bawl like a baby. Just crying his heart out.

So his sister was wrong by that much, he wasn't all a man yet, not by no means. But the kind of life I've led, I've heard a few people cry their hearts out, and you get to be kind of expert in them things. And I judged that this cry was about Hoot's last.

CHAPTER 4

It stormed for two more days, not a lot more snow, but it blowed and drifted until them eight miles to Mooney looked like eight hundred.

I never seen nobody eat like them three kids. Liddie could help in the kitchen, but she wasn't used to an iron stove, and pots and pans and dishes. As fur as she could remember, they'd cooked in an iron kettle over a fireplace, and et out of tin plates, and then just rubbed them down with ashes instead of washing them.

She caught on fast and got to be real good help, except that every time she salted anything, it made her remember her pap. It appeared that old Swiverton had been a caution in his day. He made shine, and drank so much of it that he never really made money at it, and he fit with everybody, especially his wife's kin.

But after she died on him, he changed overnight. He stopped drinking and fighting with people, and vowed he'd get them kids out of the wagons before he died. It was hard for Liddie to think of him laying out there in the wagon, where he'd keep. Hard on Hoot too, but it never bothered Alice none. Nothing bothered her.

None of them kids could describe the men that had done this job. Liddie had got away too soon to see the other three up close, and all she could tell me about the one that had roped her was that he was drunk.

Neither one of them noticed horse brands, nor the kind of guns they wore, things like that. Alice, who seen the most of all four of them, couldn't remember a thing, and she seemed too happy to bother about it.

The day we knowed the storm was going to break, Ownie started for Mooney to bring back the sheriff and the preacher. Them kids had their hearts set on having their pap buried with all the trimmings, not like movers was usually buried, just spaded under beside the road somewhere. Ownie rode his own horse, leading one of mine with a harness bridle on a long rope, so he could drive one ahead of him to buck out trail.

I didn't look for him back for a couple of days, but the next afternoon, after it had cleared up, here they come. Sheriff Abe

Whipple had went to Omaha to meet some of his wife's kinfolk that had come up from the Gulf Coast, and called it a vacation. Anybody that would go to Omaha in the middle of the winter for a pleasure trip, or any other time, is mighty hard up for fun. But that's where he was.

Abe's deputy, Thad Rust, come out in his stead. The county would only pay for cheap help, but I never reckoned Thad to be as no-account as most people. He was green as a gourd, and timid about making up his mind, because Abe never spared his feelings none when he made a mistake of judgment. Thad always hoped every case would turn into a nice simple shoot-out. He reckoned he could get by that way, and it's hard to criticize a peace officer that has the guts to think that way.

Me and this preacher, Reverend Rolf Ledger, was just about raised together back in Smith County, Kansas, although I was some years older. Him and me got into some scrapes together, and I catched a bullet in one of them, and we fell out over it. Then Rolf went to the pen for a holdup he didn't commit, and got to be the assistant chaplain, and was well on the glory trail when he got pardoned.

He was the First Methodist pastor in Mooney, and a good enough one from all I heard, but I wasn't one of the lost lambs he'd rescued. I reckon I'll convert on my deathbed, like most people, when it's too late for me to miss any fun. But so far, me and religion has got along pretty well without each other; it don't miss me and I don't miss it, and I say any deal that works that well is a good deal.

Rolf and Thad was married to sisters, the Venaman girls, and both girls was expecting to drop babies, Thad's in the early summer and Rolf's in the late. You never seen two seriouser young men in your life than the ones Ownie brung out with him. And the way I sized it up, I might be getting rid of my problem, but them movers' kids sure wasn't solving theirs.

"What should I do, Rolf?" Thad said, after he had looked the situation over, and seen it was just as bad as Ownie had said it was.

"I know what I'd do," Rolf said. "I'd borry Pete's wagon and team, and haul the body and these kids back to Mooney, and then find places where the kids can stay. That's what I'd do if it was me."

"I was thinking along them lines myself, but Abe is sure to say I should of shipped them to Denver or somewhere. I never had no case like this before," Thad said.

They went back the same day. It was pitiful to see them leave. Alice didn't realize it was her pap rolled up in one of my tarps in the wagon. She set there laughing and talking to herself, and at the last minute she had to jump out and go throw her arms around V.G. and say a special good-by to him.

They say dogs can tell when a person is insane, and their hair stands on end, but they won't bite. That's the way it was with V.G., except his hair didn't stand on end.

Finely they was gone, Ownie leading the way, just about tongue-tied because he couldn't curse in front of the minister, and there's no harder handicap to put on a man who has to break trail through the snow. Liddie kept waving to me until the wagon was out of sight, but Hoot just set there staring at his pap, and Alice kept chuckling and weaving her fingers together and talking like she had some kind of a secret.

I was glad to put this whole proposition out of my mind. All I want is to be left alone, and it's a good rule for somebody in my position to live by, and here I had almost got mixed up in one of the rottenest murders ever committed. It was damned if I did, damned if I didn't. I didn't want the law down on me and I sure didn't want them blowholers down on me any more than they already was.

They got back to Mooney late that night, in bright moonlight, but a big crowd of people had stayed up to wait for them. Rolf got four or five men to go to the graveyard and hack out a grave below the frostline, which was nearly forty inches down, so they could have a morning burial. That took until daylight.

They had the funeral at nine-thirty in the morning. There wasn't time to heat up the church for it, and no need anyway. They just carried him up the hill to the graveyard on foot, Thad Rust leading the way, and Rolf following the body with the three Swiverton kids.

Liddie and Hoot never shed a tear. Alice went skipping and hopping along over the ice and through the snow, clapping her hands together and talking to herself, saying, "Oh my oh my oh my, suchy purty town, look at all the purty houses, ain't never *seed* suchy purty town, oh my oh my oh my." She was such a little beauty and looked so happy that she had a lot of them people crying, even old men.

They didn't take time to make Pap a coffin, and Hoot said the old man would of felt kind of tight in a box anyway. They just laid him down in my own quilt, without asking what I thought about it or anybody else, and Rolf read the service over him as short as he could, because Hoot and Liddie was about to play out.

He took all three kids home with him for his wife to watch, while him and Thad went to see Andy Obers, the county judge, to ask what to do about the kids.

"Nothing you can do about the oldest girl," Andy said. "She's above the age of consent and has been emancipated by her father's death. She has all the rights and privileges of an adult except voting and making contracts. If she wants to join somebody in having a guardian *ad litem* appointed for her, a court can deem her a legal infant. But if she won't join in the petition, the only way you can overcome the presumption of emancipation is by showing she's a public charge, or a menace to morals."

"She won't take kindly to having a guardeen," Thad said. "Who would be the guardeen, anyway?"

"Why, you," Andy said, "as a county officer. You have the responsibility *de facto* for all three."

"Let's go on to some other idee then," Thad said.

Andy said the next best thing was have the two young ones made wards of the court, and he'd appoint Thad to find places where they could work out their keep. Thad wanted to get shet of the whole affair before Abe got back. It was his idee that they could ship the kids to some orphanage in Denver or somewhere.

"The only way to do that," Andy said, "is to get them to consent to it, and appoint you guardian *ad litem* for all three, and then you petition me for commitment."

"Judge, by God I expected better of you than this!" Thad said. "You know what Winnie will say, in her condition, if I'm guardeen of a girl seventeen years old, built like that girl."

"The law puts up fences around widows and orphans. There's a reason for everything," Andy said.

"I never seen a fence without a gate, nor a law without a loophole by God," Thad said. "What I want you to do is find me that loophole."

"You hire yourself a lawyer," Andy said. "I ain't scouting out no loopholes for you."

"Oh sure, and you know what Winnie will say if I go spending money on lawyers," Thad said.

Winnie was his wife, and used to a lot more than Thad could provide her on a deputy's pay. They said that her father, Cal Venaman, had four cents of the first nickel he ever earned, and had wore the other one cent out counting it, and while this may be a severe judgment, it wasn't no libel.

Thad had to go to Jimmy Drummond, who said he got two dollars each for drawing up two petitions. One was to have Thad named guardian *ad litem* to all three kids, and the other was a motion to commit them to an orphanage in Denver. Andy looked the petitions over and ordered that the infants in question be brought before him.

Rolf went down to the parsonage and got Hoot and Liddie and Alice, and took them to the courthouse. Andy asked them how they felt about going to an orphanage in Denver. Alice just smiled at him and said she thought it would be nice, everybody was so nice to her.

"I ain't going to no orphanage," Liddie said, "and neither is my brother. Our pap is buried in the ground here. There ain't no wheels between us and that ground, and here me and Hoot aim to stay."

"Miss Swiverton, can you read and write?" Andy said.

"You mean me?" Liddie said. "I kin read and write a little. But I ain't going to sign nothing, and I ain't going to no orphanage."

Andy chuckled and said she had spirit all right, and was within her rights. He would deny the commitment and hold the petition for appointment of a guardian *ad litem* in his desk until Thad come up with a fresh idee.

Thad and Jimmy Drummond went out into the hall to talk it over, while Andy kept the kids in his warm courtroom. "Thad, they hold the trump aces," Jimmy said. "Andy is perfectly right in not overruling the minors' natural and rightful desire to remain near the family grave."

"A hell of a narrow gate you found for me," Thad said. "I reckon you figure you took me for four dollars."

Jimmy Drummond was as good a lawyer as there was west of the Mississippi, and he had his pride, and he was getting on in years, and he didn't enjoy going out in the cold just to have some young badge-heavy deputy scold him. He said, "You asked me to draw you up two petitions, and I done it, I drafted them. Now if you ask my advice on a better way to do it, it'll cost you five dollars but will get you out of a pack of trouble. That's my last offer, take it or leave it, and let Andy *order* you to do whatever he's a mind to."

"Jesus, that's nine dollars already," Thad said. "But what else can I do? Go ahead."

Jimmy drawed up two more petitions. One declared Liddie emancipated, and the other one made her guardian *ad litem* for the other two. Thad just about cried when he seen how simple it was, and was still going to cost him nine dollars.

Andy declared court open, and he swore Liddie in as a witness. She testified her parents was both dead, and that she was the oldest surviving member of the family, and that she was willing and able to act as guardeen to her brother and sister. Andy ruled that way, and held Thad responsible for finding them places to stay. Then he said it would cost Thad a filing fee of one dollar for each petition, a total of four dollars, including the two he had turned down.

"Great God, why don't you put my feet in a vise and be done with it?" Thad said. "I only got $2.35 on me, and I'm supposed to bring home some beans and things out of that."

"I reckon you've suffered enough, Acting Sheriff Rust," Andy said. "I'll give you some free advice that would cost you at least five dollars if you retained private counsel. You can put in a claim to the county for this whole bill, and they'll have to pay it. The statute makes the county responsible, and if Abe Whipple gives you any trouble about it, you tell him to see me."

Thad felt better then, and him and Rolf rustled around to find places for them kids, and got them all located by dark. He thought Liddie would be the one to give him the most trouble. There was plenty of places would take her, all right, for the wrong reasons.

Most respectable homes don't want a mover's kid around, specially a grown woman in every way except knowing how to eat politely, and do housework, and keep herself clean, and so on. After growing up in a wagon, Liddie wasn't much better than a savage in her manners.

There was this rich old maid, Liz Saymill, whose brother had been a loan shark, and got murdered for six hundred dollars, and left her every cent. She needed help and could afford it, but she couldn't keep a girl because her girl had to milk the cow and take care of her buggy horse, because she wasn't going to pay no hired girl eight dollars a month and her keep, and then hire somebody to care for her livestock besides.

"I have no choice, have I?" she said. "She'll have to bathe and put on clean clothes before she comes into my house, however—mark you well that!"

"She ain't got no other clothes, ma'am. She's just barely covered up as it is," Thad said.

"Take her to the store and tell Buck to fit her out and send me the bill, and if he tries to palm off the purple junk he bought to cheat the Indians with, only they was too smart to buy it, I'll have his life," Liz said.

Buck had to guess Liddie's measurements, because he sure wasn't going to go feeling around her with no tape measure, not with all the attention Liddie was getting, but he sent her to Liz with a whole paper sack of new clothes. Liz didn't even shake hands with her.

"What's in the bag, child?" she said. "Let's see how he has outfitted you. Come, come, open it up!"

Liddie opened it up and let it all fall on Liz's carpet, and then she fell down on her knees too. She wouldn't even touch the things, just point to them.

"Shoes, real shoes, not moccasins," she said. "What's this, some kind of underclothes? I never had nothing but floursack pants underneath before. Oh look, ma'am, what's these things?"

"They're bandeaus, or as some people say, brassieres," Liz said.

"Stockings too," Liddie said. "Oh, ma'am, I cain't, it ain't fitten, I never had nothing like this, it'd be a sin for somebody out'n a wagon to dress so, trash like me—"

Thump, that was as far as she got, and Liz leaned over and rapped her on the head with her knuckles. "You look here now," she said, "what's your name?"

"Liddie Swiverton," Liddie said.

"It is *not* Liddie, it's Lydia, and Swiverton is an honest English name, and you are *not* trash, no one in this house is *ever* trash; now go take a bath and put on your new things and let me look you over," Liz said.

Liddie dragged the washtub into the kitchen, and had her bath, and managed to struggle into the clothes somehow, and even combed her hair out with her fingers. She come into the room where the old lady was sewing away in her rocking chair.

"Ma'am, how do I look?" she said.

"Why, child, you're beautiful!" Liz said. "Why, Lydia, your beauty is something to live up to, indeed it is, we must make a lady of you to go with all that gracious good looks. For manners and speech are a part of beauty too, Lydia. You must speak properly and act like a lady."

Liddie dropped to her knees beside the old lady's chair, and folded her hands together, and said, "Oh, ma'am, will you learn me manners, and how to talk? Will you?"

"I shall *teach* you, and you will *learn*, lesson number one," Liz said. "That fool of a Buck, I shall have his life yet, what did he think you were to wear while you're washing these things? Why didn't the man send along a change of clothing for you?"

"I kin sew, ma'am, the teeniest stitches if I got a small enough needle. I kin broider too. My mammy learned me—" Liddie said.

"Your mother *taught* you, and you *learned* it," Liz said. "Very well, you shall sew too, but first we'll have Buck send over another outfit. Now your name is Lydia, not Liddie, and I'm Miss Liz to you, are we clear on that?"

"Yes, Miss Liz," Liddie said.

Old Liz leaned over and put her old wrinkled cheek against the girl's clean black hair, and cried a couple of tears, and said Liddie was as bright and sincere as she was lovely, and God moved in a mysterious way His wonders to perform.

That took care of Liddie. Rolf and Samantha Ledger took in Hoot, so he could help them fix up the old parsonage before it caved in. Samantha told Hoot he'd have snow on his bed, but he said he was used to that. The parsonage wasn't much, sure enough, but they'd never had a preacher before with a wife that had been a Venaman, and there looked to be a lot of changes around there before the year was out.

Alice went to Bridey Millsap. Bridey's husband, Elias Millsap, had homesteaded early in the Kincaid game, about five miles from Mooney. He farmed it until he proved up, and then went to brokering horses, and done real good at it, and left 160 acres and quite a bit of money in the bank when he left Bridey a widow. Her real name was Bridget, but everybody called her Bridey, even the men she hired to keep the brokerage business going.

Bridey was a big fat easygoing woman, hard in a horse trade all right, but soft about kids. She hadn't never had no kids of her own, and here she seen a chance to get a pretty fourteen-year-old girl to raise, and it seemed like a blessing from heaven. She wasn't worried because Alice's mind had quit on her. It'd come back, she said.

"She's the sweetest thing, so eager to please, so cheerful to have around!" she told Rolf, when he went out a couple of days later to see how the girl was getting along. "She's already better. As soon as she feels *safe* again, her mind will come back."

The day after Rolf went out to see Alice, Abe Whipple got back to town. He went over the whole case with Thad, and then with Rolf, and then with Andy Ober. He said he reckoned they'd made the best of a bad job, although the county commissioners was going to raise hell at the expense of burial and court costs, but just let them.

"And, Thad, I promise you one thing sure," Abe said. "Sooner or later, I'm going to catch up with the men that done this. I'm going to exercise restraint and not shoot them like I would mad dogs. I'm going to save them for Andy to sentence to death, yes sir I am, and I'm going up to watch them swing, now that's a promise."

Not fifteen minutes after he said that, one of Bridey Millsap's hired hands rode in and asked Abe to come out to the place, and bring Dr. Tattnal with him because Alice was sickly.

Abe and the doctor went right out. They couldn't get Alice to say nothing, in fact she was already so feverish she thought she was floating, and they had to hold her down on the bed.

"She's been losing blood and didn't even know it, poor child," Bridey said. "She left a trail behind her wherever she went, and she wouldn't let me examine her, and pshaw, all the livestock I've handled, inside and out! I'm afraid she's a very sick little girl."

Them movers is strange, they live like pigs in some ways, and they'll go behind a little old bush that wouldn't hide a setting hen's nest when they have to squat down. But they're powerful narrow-minded about nakedness, like Hoot was, and there wasn't nobody going to take that girl's clothes off and look at her body, no sir!

Doc Tattnal had to chloroform her to examine her, and he took one look and said, "God receive her kindly, them wasn't men, them was ravening beasts, filthy ghouls, accursed and bewitched fiends out of hell, and they have killed this child." He was right. She was just all tore to pieces, and diseased besides, and was dead in four days, poor little tyke.

CHAPTER 5

Abe Whipple suffered about as much as anybody, because it was his county, and he run it his way, and it was his fault this had happened. There couldn't nobody talk him out of it, he was to blame. Somebody told him the Lord put the blowhole there to blemish the earth, the state, and the county, and maybe it was all a part of His plan.

"Then it was part of His plan for me to be sheriff, and I let Him down," Abe said. "What can you do with a blowhole? You can't knock it down, or burn it up, or wash it out, or move it away. But you can make it so hot that even a prairie dog won't hang out there, and that's where I failed. Well I never will again. There'll be nothing but dead blowholers camped there from now on, and they'll be under the sand not on it."

Alice was buried out of the church on a Sunday morning, with the best winter weather Colorado could put out. You couldn't get me into a church with a warrant most of the time, but when Rolf Ledger asked me to be a pallbearer for this little dead girl, I just couldn't squeeze out. The others was Bill Weedon and Bill Seek and Otis Paxton, all single men, and not one of them a churchgoer.

It was just Rolf's way of showing us what our lives could lead to, besides showing this little dead girl all the reverence the town could spoon out. I keep calling her a little girl, although she was fourteen when it happened, and many a woman is wife and mother at that age. But if you could of seen her in her coffin, you'd understand. She didn't weigh no more than one cent's worth of soap, and she laid there smiling like she was having a happy dream, with a white ribbon in her hair that Bridey Millsap bought. She looked like she might wake up any minute, and want a mug of fresh warm milk right out of the cow, and some fresh homemade bread.

You could just cry to see her, and the two Bills did, and both of them stone sober. Bill Seek cried all the time when he was drunk, but nobody ever seen Bill Weedon shed a tear before or after. Rolf made a short sermon of it, Suffer the little children to come unto Me, and forbid them not, for of such is the Kingdom of Heaven.

He said, "In her innocence, this child was slain by four ravening wolves, and her clean heart never knowed their vileness. Well, she knows it now, because where she sets now, nothing is hidden from her forgiving eyes, and all ends, as well as all beginnings, are knowed to her."

He said, "The merciful God warns us not to take vengeance. He told us to love our enemies, and I'm trying, oh Lord, I'm trying to obey Thee, and turn my other cheek, and repay evil with good. Lord Thou *knowest* how hard I'm trying, or I'd be out with a six-gun instead of up here preaching Thy stern word."

He said, "The sin of vengeance is a snake, and a lively one at that, and if you chop it in two, like as not them two pieces will become two snakes, and you've got two serpents to fight instead of one. Neighbors, let's look this serpent in the eye right now, and instead of fogging out to lynch somebody, let's try to figger out how the Lord handles these things. Because vengeance is His'n, not ours, and His way is the right way."

He said, "We can go this far, neighbors, in laying our wrath on the heads of this child's tormentors. Let's keep in mind that this girl is up there with the Source of all wisdom and knowledge. Nothing is hid from her forever more, and the earth is only a grain of sand to her."

He said, "Wherever them four murderers is on this grain of sand, I want them to know her eyes are on them, no they can't hide from *her*, not if they dig a hole clean to the center of the earth. Killing's too good for them, and we know it, so let us unite in a wish for a punishment far worse—that this girl's all-seeing eyes follow them until they cry out in torment for death, and can't die until they have suffered as they made her suffer, only worse."

Rolf had heard a sermon like that when he was assistant chaplain in the Kansas pen, and some dirty rat of a prisoner had killed another prisoner, and nobody knowed who done it, and they was about to have a riot. It calmed them convicts down real quick, the idee of a dead man's eyes follering his murderer no matter where he hid. A couple of nights later, the murderer went out of his head and gave himself away, and began yelling that he done it and was so guilty and ashamed, and a few of the others murdered him mercifully, and the riot never did get going.

The important thing about that sermon, though, as I seen it, was that Rolf was the first to understand just how ignorant and innocent them three movers' kids was. When he said Alice never knowed what happened to her, that was the plain truth, and neither did Hoot and Liddie understand. How people can grow up so ignorant is hard to understand, but they live a queer life in them wagons.

You expected Liddie to show up looking pretty good for the funeral, with Miss Liz to take care of her, but the marvel was how Hoot looked, as tame as he could be. Rolf and Sammie had a little trouble with him. Sammie knowed only two ways of doing things, her way and the wrong way, and she set out to shine this boy up overnight. Hoot said he never seen so much soaping and toweling in his life, and if she thought he was that dirty, why did she let him in the house?

Rolf told him it wasn't nothing personal, it was just the way folks lived in town. Hoot said he had lived in a town once, not as big as Mooney, but it had a store and a card room, and he never had to wash up there.

"Hoot, you've got to put up with it," Rolf said. "Once you get used to being good and clean, you won't be comfortable when you're dirty."

"Then what's the use of it?" Hoot said. "You're dirty a lot more than you're clean, and you'll just make yourself that much more uncomfortable."

It seemed to Rolf that this kid was trying to find out who was boss, so he said, "Do as you please, Hoot, but don't be surprised if it gets you knocked on your butt."

"By who?" Hoot said. "I never seed the day a preacher could knock me on my butt."

Rolf knocked him on his butt, and they got to be good friends again, and Hoot didn't cause no more trouble until Sammie told him he had to get his hair cut for his sister's funeral. Hoot had been past the barber shop, and had seen the men in there getting shaved and their hair cut, and the idee just scared him to death. The only haircuts he ever had before was when it got long enough to hang in his eyes, his pap hacked it off with a knife.

"The barber will teach you how to comb and part it," Sammie said, "and Rolf will buy you a comb of your own, and from now on, you comb it every time before you come to the table to eat."

"The hell I will," Hoot said, "and you cain't make me."

"The hell I can't," Sammie said. "Either you get it cut or I'll singe you like a chicken."

She opened up the stove and picked up a piece of wood by the end that wasn't burning, but Hoot just laughed at her, until she rammed the burning end into them long lank black tangles of his. Down he went on his knees. You know how burning hair stinks, well that little old leaky house was letting smoke out until you'd of thought the livery barn was on fire.

"Oh, Goddlemighty, save me, Reverend, save me!" Hoot hollered. "This woman of yourn is burning me up."

Rolf was outside mending something on the house, because that parsonage was so limber it leaned in every wind, and the day never passed that something fresh didn't break down. He loped in panting, and seen Hoot down on his knees screaming, and Sammie stabbing at him with that burning stick of firewood.

"Lord God of hosts, are you a savage, woman?" he yelled at her.

"No," Sammie said, "but he is, and he's going to take fifteen cents and get his hair cut or I'll singe it off."

She stood back with her stick, and let Rolf make up his own mind, and he knowed there was times you could argue with her and times you couldn't. He said, "Hoot, you come out loser this time. I'll go with you and get my own hair cut at the same time, although I just had it cut last month, and I can ill spare another fifteen cents."

Hoot's spirit was broken. He slunk down with Rolf and got his hair cut, and learned to part it on the left, and come home with lilac water all over it. Sammie had put supper on the table, and was so sick she was ready to puke from the smell of cooking, because being a contrary woman by nature, she had her morning sickness in the afternoon.

"My goodness, where's Hoot, and who is this handsome gentleman you brought home to supper?" she said to Rolf.

Hoot grinned and looked sillier than ever, which proves Sammie was a good winner, and that's a lot more important than being a good loser usually. You take a woman who can take that much trouble for an ungrateful brat out of a mover's wagon when she's about to turn inside out from the afternoon morning sickness, you've got a thoroughbred.

Hoot looked more man than boy at the funeral, even when he cried a little, but most of it went over his head. The same with Liddie. Maybe they thought them four miscreants wrung their sister's neck.

Rolf throwed us a signal, and me and Otis and the two Bills stood up to start toting the coffin down the aisle. Liz Saymill come up to Rolf just as he come down from the pulpit and said she wanted to talk to him, and later wouldn't do.

"Your sermon pointed up a worse tragedy, the ignorance of these children, Reverend," she said. "I fear I can't accept the responsibility for Lydia any longer. She'll be eighteen soon, and she has no more knowledge of life than a child of three."

Rolf wanted to get on with his chores, but with Liz, a problem was something to be solved, and right now, not when you got around to it. He said, "Well then, Miss Liz, find some other home for her, that's my suggestion."

"Another home for her?" Liz said. "No one else will take her, or I wouldn't have her in the first place."

"Then turn her out in the street," Rolf said. "Either that, or teach her what she needs to know. What other choice do you have, Miss Liz?"

"I? Why good God, I'm a maiden lady!" Liz said, and she just glittered her eyes at him.

"If you know enough to know she's ignorant," Rolf said, "you know what she's ignorant of. I have to get up here every Sunday and warn people of the agonies of Hell, too, and I never been there. Just because you have got no personal experience with a thing don't mean—"

"Drop it," Liz said. "I'll make out. One thing about us Methodists, we never yet let ignorance come between us and our Christian duty."

Me and Otis and the two Bills toted the coffin up the aisle and out the door, with Rolf coming along behind. Just outside the front door was Ownie Cope, leaning against the wall with his boots crossed, and his jackknife in his hand, opening and closing it.

"Maybe you can set on your hind end and let the girl's eyes punish them bastards," he said to Rolf, "but I ain't, and I just thought I'd tell you."

"You're drunk, Ownie, but not drunk enough to create a scene at this girl's farewell I hope," Rolf said.

"I won't make no scene," Ownie said, "but you and me is going to have a little talk later on."

He stood there with his old dirty hat in his hand while we packed the coffin down to where Abe Whipple had formed up the Honor Society of the Native Sons and Daughters of Mooney County in an honor guard. They was all in their purple sashes, with Abe carrying the flag with the initials and Founded 1862 sewed on in white letters, although Abe was born in Canada or Michigan, he wasn't sure which side of the line.

"Tin-*chun!*" Abe said, and thumped his pole on the frozen ground, and them old Native Sons creaked their old bones and shuffled their feet, and we slid the coffin on the running gears of the wagon, and then lined up two on each side, me and Bill Weedon on one side, and Bill Seek and Otis on the other side.

Every time there's a funeral, everybody says they've got to fix the road to the graveyard, but nobody ever does, and we had to walk beside and hold the coffin on the wagon. Sammie Ledger leaned on Hoot's arm like he was a grown man, and Liddie walked along with her arm around Liz Saymill to comfort her instead of being comforted, and you never seen two handsomer people.

There was a lot of milling around while people went to their buggies and wagons, and Abe said, "Fall in," and the Native

Sons formed up in double file, and off we went. Rolf had this beautiful mare that he rode on his pastoral chores, and he led her behind the rear guard, and we kind of staggered up the hill, with a couple of dogs fighting beside the road the way they do at every funeral.

Ownie Cope slouched along clear at the tail end, carrying his old dirty hat, and opening and closing his knife. If he sorrowed any, he didn't show it. He looked his usual mean self, was all.

At the graveyard we put the coffin on a pair of old castaway ropes, in case they got stuck under the coffin and had to be buried with it, and lowered that little girl into the cold frozen ground. How light she was, and how cold that old dirt did seem! Yet it was kind of like going home to her, because at least she was out of the wagon, and her pap was right next to her.

Sammie Ledger raised two geraniums in two pots, one dark red and one kind of orange, and she'd brung along two flowers. She give one to Liddie and one to Hoot, and they stepped up and dropped them in on their sister's coffin, and me and Bill Seek picked up the shovels and began throwing in the clods. I ain't got no business doing that kind of work, with a bullet in my abdomen somewhere; so in a minute, Rolf told Bill Weedon and Otis to spell us off.

We got her buried at last, and that whole town had come out to honor a little mover's child, even a few people that had no business out in cold weather. That's the kind of neighborly people they was, outside of the normal ornery streak you expect in everybody. I won't say they'd come through every time somebody got in trouble, but they would as often as not, and they had this time.

I walked back with Rolf, leading his horse. Going down the hill, Ownie Cope ranged up on the other side of Rolf, no drunker than usual, but no soberer either.

"Reverend," he said, "I ain't an expert on sermons, but one thing you said up there really puzzled me."

Rolf said, "If you spent half as much time in church as you do in saloons, I reckon you'd understand."

Ownie thought this over. "I reckon not," he said. "It don't take much to get me drunk. I can support my thirst a lot cheaper than I could my remorse, if I was a dues-paying Christian. I reckon you don't feel like explaining religion to me now, though."

"I will if I can," Rolf said, "but if you're only trying to hooraw me, Ownie, this is the wrong time and place."

Ownie stopped, and Rolf stopped to face him, and Ownie said, "You said if you wasn't trying to turn the other cheek, you'd be out with a six-gun. What I want to know is, *where the hell would you be with it?* Nobody else knows who to shoot. What do you know that we don't know?"

"What are you hinting at?" Rolf said.

"I ain't hinting, I'm asking," Ownie said. "You done your hitch in prison—did you meet somebody there that you later met here, that could of done this Goddamn murder?"

Rolf kind of looked off at nothing and said, "Ownie, looking back on my time in prison, I met so many that could of done it that I wouldn't know where to start naming them."

Ownie's hand shot out and took Rolf by the arm. "That ain't no answer! Who did you know in prison that you have seen *here?* Say somebody gets out, and hears that his old pard is now a preacher in Mooney, Colorado. Say he rides here to borry four bits from him, and maybe he can and maybe he can't.

"But one thing sure, his old pard, the Reverend Rolf Ledger, sees him and remembers him! Maybe this ex-convict goes on out to the blowhole and camps there. Maybe he's got three trail-pards out there, maybe the reason they hang around is the Reverend Rolf Ledger could help them if the son of a bitch only would. Maybe the preacher-man turned them down once too often, and they're riding back to the blowhole, and they see this mover's wagon with two girls in it—"

Ownie choked up like a schoolboy and started to cry, and had to start cursing under his breath to shut it off. Rolf said, "Ownie, I promise you one thing. If I ever have the least suspicion of where to lay hands on the men that done this,

Christian forbearance will not stand in the way of my going straight to Abe Whipple."

"Then you do know somebody," Ownie said.

Rolf shook his head. "I don't know anything," he said.

"I dare you to come right out and say like a man that you don't even *suspicion* nobody," Ownie said. And when Rolf didn't answer him, Ownie said, "Oh *shit*, you're no better than they are." He closed his knife and stumbled down the hill like a blind horse, and when old Rolf and me went on, Rolf wouldn't even look me in the eye.

CHAPTER 6

Rolf took his job mighty serious. The Catholic church was only a mission, and the bishop hadn't got around to sending out another buck nun after their last one died, and the other Protestant sects didn't flourish, and Rolf you might say had a monopoly. He was getting twenty-four dollars a month when he could collect it, plus feed for his horse, plus that shacky old parsonage, plus a fresh cow to milk, and new potatoes and garden truck in season.

A man can make out on that, but his wife was used to a lot more, and he wouldn't let her take nothing from her father, Cal Venaman. It was probably a good thing them movers' kids come along when they did, because he was running out of work. He had that town policed up pretty good, and a man like Rolf has got to have something to fight, and he was in a mood to go out missionary to the Apaches, or some other way of proving his zeal.

Rolf set about learning Hoot the things a grown man needs to know, like where babies come from, and what causes it, and all the other trouble it can cause. Liddie used to come visit Hoot every few days, and once her and Sammie got to talking about the same subject, and Sammie told Rolf that the girl was remarkably well prepared to face life in them subjects.

So maybe it wasn't just theory to Liz after all, but the past is the past, and it's her business anyway. The important thing is, she learned that girl what she had to know; yet neither Liddie nor Hoot ever seemed to realize what had been did to their sister.

Hoot was good with tools. He helped Rolf fix up the parsonage, and clean the dead dogs and old whisky bottles out of the well, and put up a new well sweep, and dig a new privy hole and move the privy. When spring come on, they never did let the weeds get a start, and he was prob'ly the first Methodist preacher in that town that could see out of his front window all the way to the street. Them weeds had discouraged other preachers pretty bad.

In May they had a family dinner one Sunday for all of Sammie's family at the parsonage. Sammie's parents, Cal and Opal Venaman was there, and Winnie and Thad Rust, her sister and brother-in-law, the deputy sheriff. After they et, while the women done the dishes, the men went out and set on some nice clean boxes that Rolf had put in the shade to set on.

Cal Venaman was a tall skinny well-dressed man. Even in his own cow camp he stayed well-dressed-looking, and Hoot was really smit at setting at the same table with the likes of him. He never had a word to say.

They just made themselves comfortable on them boxes, when Cal said, "Mr. Swiverton, may I compliment you on your appearance? You have a remarkable dignity, young man, indeed you do."

"Ha?" Hoot said.

"You're a credit to your family," Cal said, "and if my clerical son-in-law has no moral reservations about it, I should like to offer you a cigar."

"Have your fun, Cal," Rolf said.

"Well do you or don't you?" Cal said.

"If he's going to take up the weed," Rolf said, "why start him on something that can cost a nickel a day? He ain't a rich man, to go around smoking them cigars."

Cal handed Hoot a cigar and said, "Mr. Swiverton, that's an excellent five-center, and I trust it may inspire you to earn the good things of life. That's what good things are for—inspiration, not envy."

"Thank ye, sir," Hoot said.

He lit up and smiled all over. Them movers smoke early. Their mothers give them a puff of the corncob pipe for the nursing colic or the toothache, or just to shut up their crying, and by the time they're ten most kids have their own pipes. The reason Liddie and Hoot didn't, there wasn't no tobacco raised in Colorado, and anything they couldn't raise, they done without.

"Like it?" Cal said.

"Sweeter than a yam," Hoot said.

"Good!" Cal said. "You have no trade, have you? How would you like to work for me, and learn the cattle business?"

Hoot almost strangled on his cigar. "Sir, I'd love that better than anything else on earth!"

Cal looked at Rolf and said, "Have you any objections? How does the idea strike you?"

"He'll have to make a living someday," Rolf said. "So long as he goes on with his reading and writing and ciphering, I'm for it."

"Opal will teach him," Cal said. "Very well, let's consider it settled."

"Hold on there!" Rolf said. "How much did you figger to pay him?"

Cal paid his cowhands twenty-five dollars a month, extra in the haying season. He said, "Hoot's skill with tools is not in demand at the Flying V. I thought of this more as a learning apprenticeship, Rolf."

"I bet," Rolf said.

He looked at Thad and kind of grinned, and Thad squirmed on his box like he'd like to second the motion if he dared to. Cal got kind of red-faced.

"I don't need a carpenter or a mason," he said. "The lad wants to learn the cattle business, damn it!"

Rolf said, "There's always something needs fixing, and a man is earning something even if he's only shagging gates at the branding pen. How about half pay?"

That's what they agreed on. Samantha raised some hell when she heard about it, when Cal said he'd sleep in the bunkhouse and grub with the crew. Sammie said he'd learn more in the bunkhouse than he would at any branding fire, and all of it he could do without.

Rolf knowed this was a fact, but you can't keep a growing boy from learning them things anyhow, and there wasn't no bedbugs in the Flying V bunkhouse, and for all his nasty talk, Cal wasn't a hard man to work for. They made the store open up and sell them an extra change of clothes for Hoot, and he went out with Cal and Opal that same day.

It turned out just fine. Hoot was a humble, quiet kid, anxious to please, not afraid to work, and strong for his age. He had the soul of a cowboy, as the saying goes, being early to rise, first to the privy, and first to the table.

Hoot hadn't never handled horses except the old bonebags

movers have, that you drive with rope lines, and keep a prod pole in your hand. The Flying V was famous for its horses, and kept three good studs, and raised one hundred to one hundred and fifty horses to sell every year. Cal put him to helping a man he had there breaking colts.

"Hoot is an animal himself, I think," he told Rolf later. "He doesn't have a thing to learn about a horse somehow. He can get his bare hands on a range colt faster than anyone I have ever known, and once he touches it, it's his horse."

He paid Hoot a hand's full wages from the start, and pretty soon Hoot had his own saddle string, and Cal got on his tail the same as he did his regular hands, and by summer's heat, the mover's kid was a cowboy. Now you could listen to old cowboys set around all day, telling what a low-down miserable hopeless thankless job it is, only they never seen it until too late.

But nobody could of made Hoot Swiverton believe that. The only thing that stuck in his craw, he had to go to the house every evening for some lessons, and the crew teased him about that until he whipped a couple of them, and he fretted considerable until he seen it was part of the price of his job. Ruther than give up being a cowboy on the Flying V, he would of learned hemstitching.

Nothing like that for Liddie, though.

For Liddie it was just work and study, study and work, work and study. Liz Saymill said life was hard for the poor, and harder for the rich than the poor suspicioned, and you had to bluff your way to the grave by knowing how to do many things well. She learned Liddie to cook and bake and sew and make jelly, and set hens and raise garden and milk the cow, and even paint the window sashes and put back some bricks that had fell out of the chimbley.

You'd of thought Liz didn't have no feeling for the girl at all. Do this, do that. Straighten up! Don't go about humped over like a pot-lickin' dog. Pick up your feet, don't drawl your words. Look a person in the eye and smile, like you had some pride in yourself!

"I'll make a lady of you or kill you, Lydia," she said, "and as God is my witness, I wonder which!"

"Don't aim me too high, ma'am," Liddie said. "The upper the leap, the downer the tumble."

"Don't you believe that!" Liz said. "You can do anything, be anything, have anything, that you aspire to in Christian humility. You can even have it without the humility, but not in my house!"

You wouldn't of thought a girl could enjoy suchy life, but Liddie did. After the shiftless life of a wagon, she just loved having firm rules to lean on, and strong walls around her life, and somebody that thought she was important enough to nag.

Women are strong for rules in little things, at least most of the time, although when it comes to running off with the wrong man, the sensiblest of them can jump the fence, buggy and all. This was what worried Miss Liz the most, that Liddie was old enough to get into trouble, and in spite of everything she'd learned her, stayed just as innocent and helpless as the day she was born.

Some women are that way, just too trusting and good, and it's all right if they happen to trust the right man at the right time. But how often does that happen? And like Liz said, why is it the tenderest and fairest flower in the garden that always gets strangled by a big overbearing weed?

Spring stumbled along into summer, and the heat come on, and it rained on the Fourth of July and not again until the twenty-ninth of August, and the cattlemen's range and the nesters' crops just went to hell. Liddie spent an hour a day lugging buckets of water to the garden and flowers, while Liz set under the grape arbor and fanned herself and wondered if it was worth the trouble, if the Lord had lost countenance with Colorado or what.

Liddie had got into the habit of taking some flowers up to the graveyard every Saturday, and putting them on the graves of Pap and Alice, and keeping the weeds pulled so the grass could root in if it ever rained again. And it was on the twenty-eighth of August, the day before it finely rained, that Liz come running to Rolf for advice and consolation. She was more wrought up than Rolf had ever saw her, and Liz was a woman who got wrought up easy and often. . . .

It dawned on Liz that Liddie had got mighty pious about them graves all of a sudden, and in the worst hottest weather of all, was toting flowers up there just about every day. It was the way she done it, too. Seemed like it had to be about the same time every afternoon, and when it got along towards that time the girl got restless and moody and pink-faced, and could hardly wait, and then she took longer and longer to do it, and come back moodier than ever.

Liz couldn't believe Liddie was two-faced enough to be meeting no man on the sly, but she couldn't take no chance. One afternoon she just *happened* to go visiting a neighbor on the way to the graveyard, at the time Liddie was supposed to come home.

Her and this neighbor set out on the front porch with a pitcher of water from the well all afternoon, but she didn't see no sign of Liddie, yet when she got home, Liddie was already peeling the potatoes for supper, in a kind of a daze Liz thought. Liz wanted to come right out and ask her where she'd been, or whack her across the bottom with a broom, only she couldn't bring herself to do either one.

But the next day, she remembered there was another way to the graveyard, clear around town instead of through it. There was this one stretch about forty rods long, an old rundown road with a row of trees along one side, and a plum thicket on the other, and the thrashers and meadow larks nested in the plums, and the young cottontails hid in the shade there, and the grasshoppers was always sawing away like a German band.

In the hot dry summer the dust laid thick there, and this was a hot dry one, and the kids loved to splash barefoot in the dust, and whoop and holler at how hot it was, and make tracks like an elephant. Only in the afternoon it was too hot for kids even, and the birds kept to the shade, and the goldenrod and sunflowers drooped in the dust.

"I hid myself there, in all frankness," Liz said. "I stooped to spying, Reverend. I became an eavesdropper and a sneak!"

She give up her afternoon nap to do it, and stood there in the shade of them spindly old trees, what there was of it, and pretty soon, here came Liddie. Liz felt her heart just go *crack* when she seen it was Ownie Cope with her, the lowest of the low.

They wasn't doing anything, not even holding hands, not talking, just ambling along with their heads down, Ownie carrying his old dirty hat, and Liddie carrying a couple of dandelions. In her worst nightmares, Liz hadn't suspicioned it could be Ownie Cope.

"I was going to rage out like a policeman and march her back into town for all the world to behold for the slattern strumpet from the wagons that she was," Liz said, "and if Ownie Cope opened his big mouth, I was going to tell him some things no man would dare tell him without putting the muzzle of a gun between his eyes first."

"Why didn't you?" Rolf said.

The old lady wrung her hands. "Because it looked too holy, that's why," she said.

"Holy," Rolf said. "Ownie Cope. I see. Holy."

"There are moments when one knows that God is both very good and very close," Liz said. "One knows that He made the trees, the sun, the birds that sing, the warm kindly earth under us, the bees to hum and the flowers to bloom and the hot wind to whisper. Such a moment, Reverend, found me hiding like a sneak."

"Go on," Rolf said.

"It came to me in my foolish human vanity, that if God made these things, he made them not just for me, but for Lydia and Ownie Cope too. Yes, for even Ownie Cope! And I could only hide as Adam and Eve tried to hide, and hope to God my sin would not find me out to them."

"Well did it?" Rolf said.

"No. Blessedly they went on, and I was a long time with my head bowed, let me tell you! I still feel I trespassed on something holy, and you'll never persuade me otherwise. What I want from you, Reverend, is this—how did Ownie Cope get into anything holy?"

"I sure don't know, Miss Liz," Rolf said, "but I wouldn't put nothing past the Lord. Your own heart is a better guide than I am, ma'am."

"I knew that," Liz said, "but it's a comfort to hear you admit it. I'll do the best I can by that girl and trust in His wisdom to protect her, for I can't."

Rolf went looking for Ownie, and found him across the crick, where the old red-light district used to be, until Abe Whipple was forced to abolish it by decree. Ownie was setting on an old pole fence, with his heels hooked over a pole, and his hat down over his eyes, carving a little wooden dog out of a piece of wood.

"Howdy," Rolf said, and clumb up beside him, and hooked his heels over too.

Ownie shoved his hat back and said, "Howdy. I don't reckon this is an accidental meeting, Reverend."

"Not in no way," Rolf said. "Liz Saymill is some upset about you meeting Liddie at the graveyard."

"She is, is she," Ownie said.

"Yes, and she's got every right. I wish every man well, Ownie, but you got to admit you're no bargain for any woman," Rolf said.

"You never said correcter words, Reverend," Ownie said. He eased himself off'n the fence and closed his knife up and put it away, and said, "Listen, would you believe me if I said I never spoke a word to that girl that the whole town couldn't hear?"

"Sure, I'd believe that," Rolf said. "If you tell me that, I believe it, sure."

Ownie nodded soberly. "I don't want to make her no trouble. I won't see her no more, Reverend. I wasn't getting nowhere with her nohow," he said.

"I should hope not," Rolf said.

Ownie didn't even seem to hear him. He said, "Reverend, does the name Cappy Sanno mean anything to you?"

Rolf felt he had a kind of a buzzing in his ears, Ownie had

changed the subject on him so fast. He said, "No it don't but it sounds a lot like Capistrano, so maybe you heard wrong."

"Capistrano," Ownie said. "What's that?"

"It's a place in California," Rolf said. "Why?"

"Nothing," Ownie said. "Well, I won't make no more trouble for Liddie. I didn't have no idee I was! Why I wouldn't harm that girl for anything, why what do you think I am anyway?"

"I wonder myself sometimes," Rolf said. "What are you, tell me."

"The son of a steamboat whore," Ownie said, and he went slouching away, and didn't look back, and Rolf felt so sorry for him he didn't know what to do. He knowed that Ownie was in love with Liddie, but he wasn't going to bother her no more because he felt too low-down for her, even if she had come out of a mover's wagon. People can get into some of the worst messes that way.

Rolf dropped in on Liz Saymill that evening, and told her not to worry. He said that Ownie was smitten with Liddie, but an unexpected contrary streak of decency had cropped up in him, and he'd stay away from her instead of getting a job and quitting drinking.

"Even when people do the right things," he said, "often as not they do them for the wrong reasons, and it don't make my work no easier, let me tell you."

Liz cried a little. "It seems such a shame that anything so holy can't survive in our climate," she said. "And it was holy, it was!"

Liddie come in then, just as pretty as she could be with that olive skin of hers kind of flushed, and her black eyes snapping. Rolf talked around with her a few minutes, trying to think of a way to lead up to it.

Some things just can't be led up to. He finely had to come right out and say, "Liddie, I wonder if the name Capistrano means anything to you?"

Liddie turned white, and her eyes popped wide open, and she put her hands to her cheeks. "That's it!" she screamed. "That's it, that's what one of the men was called that killed

Pap and Alice. Capistrano, that's the name they called him!"

Rolf helped Liz quiet the girl down, but when he went to look for Ownie Cope, to remind him that Vengeance is mine saith the Lord, he couldn't find him nowhere. The reason he couldn't, Ownie was at my place for almost a week, staying drunk as he could, and in between times as poison mean as he could be. And he could be as poison mean as anybody I ever knowed.

CHAPTER 7

It was *so* hot you had trouble getting to sleep before two or three in the morning, and more trouble getting up. I got up one morning, and Ownie was setting there at the kitchen table, with a pencil and a paper, sober as a judge.

"I'll be off your hands today, Pete," he said. "Wonder where a man could find a job?"

"A lot of good men are wondering that," I said.

"I reckon so," Ownie said. "Pete, what do you think I could get for my horse?"

"Last spring I'd of said a hundred and fifty dollars, today I don't know, maybe as much as a hundred," I said.

"That's about what I figgered," he said.

"How are you going to find a job if you sell your horse?" I asked him.

"I ain't sure what I'll do," he said, and that was all I could get out of him.

He didn't have the shakes like a lot of men do when they sober up, and he wasn't in what I'd call a real mean mood, and he didn't seem nervous at all. He thanked me for letting him lay around there drunk as a hog, which he never done before, and left real early in the morning.

That was the day Charley Parker's Roofed Lazy 8 outfit turned over five hundred cows Charley had sold to Cal Venaman. Abe Whipple had a fit when he found out Cal was going to take possession in Mooney. Ownie got to town in time for Abe to do all his complaining to him.

"That's a cowman for you, what does he care how much trouble he causes; well, by God, the first wild range cow that gets loose in this town is a dead cow," he said.

"I don't blame you, Abe," Ownie said. "Them days is gone forever."

Them cattlemen used to just turn a herd loose and laugh their heads off to see it tear through a town, running over yards and tangling up in clotheslines, with women climbing trees and wagons getting turned over and now and then a kid killed. Abe had stopped that in Mooney by shooting cows down and then daring them to do anything about it.

A cattleman didn't care if you shot up his help. He could

always hire another cowboy, but a dead beef cost him money. Many a sheriff would of been run out of the country for standing up to the cattlemen the way Abe had, but he had his own system. When the cattlemen was against him, he made sure he had the townfolks and the nesters on his side, and when he had to bear down on the town people or the nesters, he first made friends with the cowmen.

Abe and Thad showed up all garnished up with guns, each with a .30-30 carbine in his saddle boot. Thad looked like he was waiting to mount the gallus to be hung, if Abe took a notion to order him to shoot one of his father-in-law's cows.

Cal had eight men, including Hoot Swiverton, when he come into town. He laughed his head off when he seen Abe and Thad armed like a Mexican revolution.

"Why shoot, this is just a handful of tame cows," he said. "Four men could eat them alive."

"I hope you're right, Cal," Abe said. "For your sake, I do devoutly hope it."

"Have you ever known me to be wrong?" Cal said.

He tied his horse and walked into the store where he was to meet Charley Parker, and Abe choked a little, and then he said, "Have I ever knowed him to be wrong, and, by God, he meant it just the way it sounded, can you beat that for gall?"

"He ain't no worse than Charley Parker," Thad said. "That ain't family loyalty, either, because I don't feel none. That Roofed Lazy 8 outfit is a corker."

Charley loved to put on a show too. He always had men stumbling around over each other out there, and when he come into town, it was like his own private army. The range war days was long since gone in Mooney County, but them old customs die hard, and Charley was old enough to eat with his knife and live in the past.

Ownie Cope had worked for Charley two-three times, and could of run his outfit for him if he was a mind to, because Ownie made a good hand. But he was a restless one, and sometimes short-tempered, and as liable as not to blow up and tell Charley to go to hell over nothing.

Charley left the herd a couple of miles out of town to the

east, with four men to hold them, and rode into town with five men to meet Cal. They loved an audience, and it wouldn't of been no pleasure at all just to close the deal out there at the holding ground. No, the common people had to see the leather bag of gold change hands, and the papers signed, and the cigars swapped, or it wasn't sacred.

Charley was a big old fat man, foul-mouthed and ignorant, and Cal didn't care for him at all most of the time. But he was necessary for this ceremony, so Cal waited in the store until Charley flourished up and tied his horse and went inside.

They closed their deal on the end of the counter in the store, and swapped their cigars, and Charley throwed Cal's leather bag of gold to one of his men to tote, like this was small change to him. Abe come in the door then, and wanted to know how much longer this opera was going to go on, with five hundred wild cows just a sprint away.

Cal picked out four of his men, and said, "You go ahead and start the herd home. We'll catch up with you in a few minutes. Well thank you, Charley, and so long."

"Thank you, Cal, and so long to you," Charley said. "Let's go home, boys."

Hoot was disappointed at not getting picked to help drive the herd. He wanted the people in Mooney to see he was all cowboy and a yard wide, but at least he'd been a witness to the old trail's-end rites, and it was something he could tell his grandchildren.

Charley come out of the store with his men, and one of them was this fellow by the name of Scotty Dundy, who had come from Scotland years ago, and had this beautiful tenor voice. He was a big brawny man that loved to swagger, so he come out of the store singing, letting his R's roll like taters on a cellar door:

Flow gently, sweet Afton
Amang thy green braes,
Flow gently, I'll sing thee
A song in thy praise.

My Mary's asleep by
Thy murmuring stream.
Flow gently, disturb not
Her slumbering dream.

Scotty was vain about his voice, and he could just make you wet your pants when he cut loose sometimes. He took off his hat and swung it almost to the ground in a big stylish bow, when he reached the bottom step and the end of the song at the same time.

Up there behind him, Hoot Swiverton was just coming out of the door, and he looked like he had seen a ghost, or at least heard one.

Hoot let out a long whimpering kind of a squeal, not words just a regular old squeal, and ran down the steps. The nearest horse was Abe Whipple's, with a .30-30 sticking out of the boot. Abe was maybe a dozen feet away, and the only man there quick-minded enough to see what Hoot meant to do.

"No you don't!" Abe yelled, and jumped for the kid. But Hoot yanked the .30-30 out, and took off the safety, and snuggled the gun up against his shoulder, and come around to draw a bead on Scotty Dundy. Nobody ever had to learn a mover's kid how to handle a rifle, and Scotty wasn't but a few steps away.

Abe hit him just as he fired. The slug caught Scotty in the meat of his right leg, about halfway between the hip and the knee. Hoot was whimpering and crying and cursing and trying to hang onto the gun for another shot, and Abe was trying to take it away from him, when the second shot went off.

This one took Abe's hat off and creased him a little, and down he went, and then Ownie hit Hoot from behind and twisted the .30-30 out of his hand. Thad Rust got hold of Hoot and pulled him back and asked him what in tarnation got into him.

"He killed my sister and he killed my pap!" Hoot screamed. "Listen to how funny he talks! I remember, I remember! Well I got even with one of the sons of bitches."

Somebody run for Doc Tattnal, while Ownie and Thad was throwing this kid down and setting on him. It was like holding a full-grown puma. Abe Whipple stumbled up, bleeding down the side of his face, and Scotty Dundy was over there groaning that he was murdered, assassinated, shot from behind by a cowardly Flying V ambusher.

"Cal, take your men and get out of town, everybody but Hoot," Abe said. "You go one way, and Charley, you take your men and go the other, everybody but Scotty, he can stay here until Doc sees to him."

"I wouldn't stay in your filthy town," Scotty said. "Somebody bring me my horse and help me on him."

Abe got them out of town without no more trouble. Even Cal Venaman was too surprised to try to overrule him. Doc Tattnal come up and made Abe set down on the steps while he took eight or ten stitches in his scalp.

Abe set there and let Doc sew him up. He said to Hoot, "Son, you wild little son of a bitch, there's no decenter man in Colorado than Scotty Dundy, what made you think he killed your sister and daddy?"

"The way he talks," Hoot said. "One of them talked the same way."

"Does he look like anybody you remember?" Abe said.

"Well no, I don't remember seeing him," Hoot said.

"Well now look what you done, you shot an innocent man and you'll have to stand trial, and when it comes to that, you shot me too," Abe said. "I ought to kick your ass clear out of Colorado, that's what I ought to do."

Hoot was still white as a ghost, and weak in the knees, and a lot more scared kid than cowboy then. "I kin still hear that man in my mind, Shurf," he said, "and that's just exactly how he sounded."

"That ain't enough to kill a man for," Abe said, "and now you know it. You go on down to the jail with Thad, and wait for me there, until this damned old clumsy fool of a doctor stops fumbling around and trying to saw my head off. All of you get out of here. Everybody out, out!"

Everybody left but Ownie and the doctor, and finely the

doctor left too, and Abe set there a minute until he got his strength back.

"Ownie," he said, "what do you think?"

"I seen them dead people," Ownie said. "Scotty couldn't of did that in a million years."

"Way I figure it," Abe said.

"Scotty might come at you just for the fun of it, or if you said something nasty about the Queen, or any good reasonable cause for a fight," Ownie said. "But he wasn't one of them murdering blowholers."

"Way I figure it," Abe said. "We'll find out that Scotty didn't have nothing to do with it."

"Likely," Ownie said, "but this still puts it up to you to bet or check, don't it?"

Abe felt around of the bandage Doc had left on his head, and cursed a little, and said, "Bet or check how?"

"Why," Ownie said, "Hoot's mind unfroze enough to give you a clue to one more man. That makes three of the four you've got a line on."

"What line?" Abe said.

"One of them talks with a Scotch brogue," Ownie said, "and one of them has been in the Kansas pen, and one goes by the nickname of Capistrano."

"How do you figure all this?" Abe said.

Ownie said, "Abe, Rolf Ledger has seen somebody he suspicions, he wouldn't admit it but he did, and where would he know that kind of a murderer except in the pen? Liddie remembered something like Cappy Sanno, and Rolf says it's more'n likely Capistrano. That was what they called one of them, either Cappy Sanno or Capistrano, and you know damn well which it was."

"I've been having a bale of wool pulled over my eyes," Abe said, "and I don't like it a damn bit! This is what happens when you do something for somebody. I put Rolf in office, I give him power and responsibility and a chance to marry money, and when he's got information on a felony in my own jurisdiction, do you think he came to me with it? I'll kiss a pig he didn't. Come on, you and me is going to see Rolf right now!"

"I'll wait for you down to the courthouse," Ownie said. "I want to see how Hoot is getting along."

Hoot was just scared stiff, was how he was getting along. He was laying on one of them bunks on his back, with his arm over his eyes, and one boot toe swinging back and forth a little. He wouldn't look up to talk to Ownie, just laid there and twitched that one foot.

Abe came back a while later, with his head about to split with the headache from being grazed with a .30 bullet. "He said yes, he did see a man he remembered from the pen," he said, "but he hadn't ever knowed his name because the man got out just about the time Rolf went in, but his nose had been busted once and healed with a dent in it, and he claimed to be a gunfighter."

"What more do you want?" Ownie said. "What are you waiting for anyway?"

"What more do I want?" Abe said. "Did it ever occur to you that maybe we've got clues to just *one* man, that's a gunfighter with a broken nose and served time in the pen, and talks with a Scotch brogue, and goes by the nickname of Capistrano? How do you know it's three men, and not just one?"

Ownie leaned over the desk and said, "Abe, by God you've got a fifteen-year-old kid in your dirty dark dank filthy jail, eating his heart out in there, and you set on your big fat rump and bring up technicalities. You'd ruther hang Hoot for it than get off your can and work."

"Ownie, what do you want me to do?" Abe said. "I know something about this business. That wasn't no gang of organized criminals. They're just no-account human skunks that happened to den up together out there at the blowhole, and they ain't ever going to be seen together again, not *ever*, because they'll be scareder of each other than of anything else. Men like that don't stick together! Now what the hell do you expect me to do?"

"You could offer a reward," Ownie said. "How much is my horse worth? At least a hundred and fifty dollars. I'll put that up."

"You mean that?" Abe said.

"You try me and see by God!" Ownie said.

Abe said, "Well, Ownie, you surprise me, you back your bluffs all right. Keep your horse. Let's go get the printer going on some dodgeroos."

They got out 1,000 of them that same day:

$500 REWARD
for EACH of the following described
members of a gang of DANGEROUS RUFFIANS:
Suspect No. 1–Speaks with a Scotch brogue.
Suspect No. 2–Nicknamed Capistrano.
Suspect No. 3–Gunfighter with bent nose,
formerly a convict in Kansas State Prison.
Suspect No. 4–No description.

THESE MEN MURDERED AN OLD MAN AND A YOUNG GIRL. THEY WILL BE ARMED AND MAY FIGHT LIKE CORNERED RATS. REWARD PAID ONLY FOR DELIVERY, ALIVE, TO THE UNDERSIGNED.

EXERCISE ALL CARE IN APPROACHING THEM!

A. H. Whipple, Sheriff
Mooney County, Colorado

"Who's going to pay the five hundred dollars?" Ownie asked.

"Nobody," Abe said. "This ain't the way to get them sons of bitches, Ownie. Oh, if I was only thirty years younger!"

"Well I am," Ownie said.

"You're what?" Abe said.

"Thirty years younger," Ownie said.

CHAPTER 8

There was a contractor building some county road, and he come into town that afternoon looking for men that could handle four-mule teams, and Ownie was the first man he hired. Ownie holed up in one of them old shacks across the crick, and done his own cooking, and never showed his face in a saloon.

He come around the next evening to see Hoot in the jail. "I'm worse than them people that killed Alice and Pap, you know that?" Hoot said. "I'll be glad when I'm dead and can forget shooting that man."

"You only say that because you never been dead," Ownie said. "Nobody knows anything about death, except that this is the wagon when it backs up to the door, all of us get in sooner or later. Shut up that kind of talk."

"Reverend Ledger says if I'm truly repentant, I'll be forgiven and can forget," Hoot said, "but I reckon he means after I'm dead, because I sure can't forget now."

"He don't know no more about it than you and me," Ownie said. "I'm going to get Jimmy Drummond to take your case as soon as he gets back from Denver, and I'll talk to Scotty Dundy the next time he's in town, and ask him how he'd like to be in jail for an innocent mistake. Scotty ain't a bad person at all, Hoot."

Hoot began to dribble tears, and said, "That's what I hear, and that's what makes it so awful, I shot a good man."

Jimmy got back, and Andy Obers called the case on some kind of preliminary hearing. The county attorney was Miles James, who claimed to be a cousin of Jesse and Frank James during the campaign, although after he got elected, he admitted this was only a family boast. Miles usually meant well, and in his favor it has to be said he wasn't much of a lawyer, and couldn't get people unjustly convicted, and not many justly convicted. But he had ambitions to run for higher office, and no prosecutor ever got very far without a few hangings on his record.

You couldn't hang a fifteen-year-old kid that had only wounded his victim, but Miles shoved in his whole stack, and charged attempted murder, and Judge Obers couldn't dismiss it. He said about a week later they could go to trial.

"No, please the court, I want sixty days," Jimmy Drummond said. "I'll have some motions to file then. I mean to raise the question of defendant's age, whether a legal infant who can't contract marriage or even buy a horse in his own name, is competent to formulate the intent to commit murder. I may even raise the doctrine of attractive nuisance, and hold the county culpable for leaving a loaded .30-30 in reach of a legal infant."

"Why I never heard such law in my life," Miles said.

"That's because you never heard much law of any kind," Jimmy said.

Judge Obers said, "You don't bluff me none, Jimmy, I've read some law myself, and if that big hulking hillbilly kid is an infant, I'm the illegitimate granddaughter of Empress Josephine. You can have your sixty days, prisoner remanded to custody of the sheriff, without bond."

Abe took Hoot down the steps to the side door of the jail, saying, "I can't remember when a prisoner has caused me more trouble than you; now let's see, sixty days, that's the last of November, well you be here about two days ahead, say the twenty-eighth. Don't come for supper, though, because you won't get any."

"Come from where?" Hoot said.

"Why out to Cal Venaman's place," Abe said. "That's where you work, ain't it? Yonder's the door and yonder's the trail, now let me miss you a while."

Hoot just about cried. He said, "I can't go there, after all the trouble I made for Cal, what if there's more trouble, and I'm to blame?"

"A range war, you mean," Abe said. "Tell Cal if I hear any such talk, to remember one thing, no matter who *starts* trouble in this county, I'm the one that *ends* it. There's always a Flying V horse in the livery barn, so go on with you boy, and don't bother me."

Hoot went and got a Flying V horse and rode out to the Flying V, and Cal greeted him like a long-lost son, and the boys in the bunkhouse made the cook bake up a sour apple pie for him. There's always a couple of expert lawyers in a bunkhouse, and they had it all figgered out. Scotty Dundy was still a British subject, and hadn't swore loyalty to the American law, and wasn't entitled to its protection, any more than a Swede or a Dutchman.

They made Hoot feel better, but the next day, Thad Rust come out there to tell about the trouble Abe got into, and Hoot was ready to go back to jail again. Judge Andy Obers sent for Abe, and asked him in open court if it was true he no longer had the prisoner in his custody.

"Why of course it ain't true, Your Honor," Abe said. "Who's going around telling crap like that?"

"Where is he?" Andy said.

"Out to the Flying V, I reckon. If you need him here for more of Miles James's foolishness, I wish you'd give a man notice," Abe said. "I've got a few other duties, you know, besides running errands for this court."

Andy almost choked. "Sheriff," he said, "this court's order was quite clear—no bail!"

"I didn't take bail," Abe said. "Ask your own Goddamn court clerk if any Goddamn bail is recorded."

"But you released the prisoner, you turned him loose in defiance of the court's orders," Andy said.

Abe said, "I done no such thing. You put him in my custody, and that's where he is, and when he's due back in this court, he'll be here. In custody don't mean I have to chain him to me, and sleep with him; a man can go to the can in privacy without dragging his prisoner along with him, can't he? Reason in all things, I've heard you say it yourself, Judge, the law is ninety-nine parts pure reason; you see, I'm quoting your own historic words right back at you. If you want this prisoner handcuffed to me twenty-four hours a day until he's due back in court, say so and I'll resign, let somebody else run this county, just let them try, that's all! I have never lost a prisoner yet, except a couple of misdemeanants that died drunk in jail, a felony prisoner never. Custody is a sacred word to me, it may be just reason to you but this Goddamn job is next to my heart, and you insult me by saying I can't be trusted with a fifteen-year-old kid unless I handcuff him and put an Oregon boot on him I suppose. Any time I lose a felony prisoner there'll be snow up to your butt in July, Your Honor. I want a ruling on *how long* the chain has to be, and do I have to *sleep* with him, and how about when I take a *bath*, lay it out for me, Your Honor."

"I don't want a speech," Andy said when he could slide a word in edgewise. "I want that prisoner."

Abe said to Thad, "All right, go out to Cal's place and tell that kid to fog it in here, this judge is snagged on one of Miles's technicalities."

"Never mind," Andy said. "I'll consider him to be in your custody, if you think you can send for him just like that, and he'll come."

"Why wouldn't he?" Abe said. "I'm the sheriff, ain't I? God help anybody that don't come when I say to."

About a week later, Ownie Cope went to Abe's house one evening and said to him, "Abe, how would you like to buy my horse?"

"That big brown gelding you ride with a three-quarter rig Rockland Myers roping saddle?" Abe said.

"How many horses and saddles do you think I own?" Ownie said. "That's the horse, and the saddle goes with him."

"Well, Ownie," the sheriff said, "you'll have trouble giving that horse away, but I'll go as high as forty dollars for him and the saddle because I feel sorry for a man so down and out he has to part with his horse and saddle."

"Last chance," Ownie said. "I'm selling today. Come nightfall, somebody else will own my horse and my three-quarter Rockland Myers roping saddle."

"I'll go as high as a hundred dollars out of pity," Abe said.

"Make it two hundred dollars and they're yours," Ownie said.

"You really mean business, don't you?" Abe said. "What will you do without a horse and saddle?"

"I thought I'd go to Denver," Ownie said. "I'm sick of the cowboy's life. What does it get you but broken bones and an

TSH level - TTK

early old age? As a kid, I worked in a locksmith shop in Kansas City. Maybe I'll go back to that and learn to be a locksmith."

"That's a good trade to have," Abe said, "but one thing sticks in my craw, that you might be going out on the vengeance trail after them murdering bastards that murdered old Swiverton and Alice."

"What made you think that?" Ownie said.

"It was a flash of inspiration, you might call it," Abe said. "Are you selling your pistol too?"

"No, I mean to keep my gun," Ownie said.

"I reckoned so," Abe said. "I'll go as high as one hundred and fifty for your horse, not a cent higher."

"Make it one hundred and sixty," Ownie said.

"All right, one hundred and sixty dollars," Abe said, "and if I've made a miscalculation somewhere, and you're going out afoot after them murderers, just keep one thing in mind, my boy. This is a public crime, not a private feud, and you've got no badge or commission or warrant. So if ever you get any wild notions, just stop long enough to ask yourself the old eternal question, whose ass now."

He didn't see Ownie again, although he heard he had went to work for a few days putting up clover hay for some nesters, a way of making money Ownie wouldn't of spit on in his reckless, rollicking prime. And then he seen old Danny Dexter wearing Ownie's old dirty hat and boots, and old Danny told him Ownie give them to him because he was wearing a cap and moccasins from now on.

Abe went to see Mrs. Deeda Meredith, who was married to Bountiful Meredith, who owned the harness shop and made saddles to order, and would tan your deerskins or bearskins for you. Deeda was an Arapahoe orphan that had been raised Methodist by some Methodist people, but she still kept in touch with the Arapahoes.

Deeda said yes, she had made Ownie some cowhide moccasins and a deerskin cap, like she made for the Araps, to make an extra dollar now and then. She said Ownie told her he was going to have to practice a lot, walking without a heel, and that was all he said.

"Deeda," Abe said, "this don't make sense."

"It sure don't," Deeda said, "and this is just when you want to watch out for Ownie Cope. An ordinary man in love is bad enough. Like Bountiful says, you get it in the head and then you ain't satisfied until you get it in the hind end, that's the madness called love. With somebody like Ownie Cope, who can predict?"

"You mean Ownie is in love?" Abe said.

Deeda said, "Abe, few women on this earth ever get loved the way Ownie loves that pretty little Liddie Swiverton. I may be an Indian, but a human heart beats beneath my dirty coppery pelt, and it just plain saddens me to see all that good pure love going to waste. You know what an Indian would do if he was in love like that?"

"Nobody knows what an Indian would do," Abe said.

"Well there you are, you say you ain't prejudiced but catch you with your guard down, and it comes out. An Indian would starve himself weak, and whet up his knives, and build a smoke fire to his gods, and then see how many he could take with him before they gunned him down," Deeda said.

"If Ownie Cope tries anything like that," Abe said, "I ain't going to gun him down, I'll just wear a pair of tugs out across his hind end. The time for that kind of raucous foolishness is long past in Mooney County."

The only other thing Abe heard, he heard that Ownie beat up on a nester who asked him why he didn't either get his hair and whiskers cut, or learn how to braid. Then it seemed to Abe that Ownie just vanished off'n the earth.

Not to me though. I come home one afternoon and seen that my quarter-strain wolf dog, V.G., was gone. His chain was still there, and Spot and Foolish was both all right, and they was always real nervous when there had been anybody around my place while I was away from it. There was only one person could get close enough to V.G. to unsnap him.

I went into the house, and here was Ownie's gun in its holster laying on my table, a real good .45 with walnut butt-plates Ownie had whittled himself, and a nice easy steady touch to the trigger, and as well kept as a lady's hands as the saying is.

Nobody but Ownie Cope could of just walked into my house that way, without Spot and Foolish tearing them to pieces.

I looked around to find what was missing, and it was just what I suspicioned, a fine double-edged hunting knife in a scabbard for wearing under your shirt. It was the best-balanced knife I'd ever owned, and Ownie used to fool with it when he was working at his drinking at my place, and could throw it clear across the common room and hit the ace of spades four times out of five. That's twenty feet.

Well it was my gun until Ownie come back, or until the Indian I had got V.G. from come to claim him, and the knife was just a dead loss. But you get philosophical as the fella says. It's part of the cost of doing business in the kind of business I was in, in the kind of country I was doing it in, and the kind of customers I had. Which Ownie was by no means the worst.

CHAPTER 9

Long before there was a tame cow in Colorado, or a tame white man, or for that matter any place west of the Missouri, there was these old-time mountain men. Trappers and hunters and gold-seekers usually, or sometimes scouts for the Army or emigrant parties, but that was just an excuse to make drinking money before they went back to their lonely ways. They was such mean, silent, solitary people that they made your average mover look downright sociable.

Their time was long gone, it went with the first settlers that dragged along a plow and a yoke of bulls to pull it, and the repeating rifle was their death sentence. Them old mountain men was sheer death with a smooth-bore musket, that always had a pet name, like Betsy or Mother Magruder or Jesus Calls. The repeating rifle evened the odds against the ace marksman, so he could no longer stand off a quarter of a mile and pick off the settlers one by one as they put their accursed plows into his wild free lonely grass, ruining things forever for him.

This is beside the point except that there was still a few of them left, or at least that's what they thought they was. They wouldn't work, and they wouldn't partner up with each other, no they just went their lonely ways, pretending the world hadn't changed, stealing what they needed when they couldn't get it some easier way, and living you might say in the past.

This was what Ownie Cope deliberately set out to be, one of them misfit mountain men with his hand against the civilized world. He had V.G. on a string when he left my place, because any mountain man that goes through a town with a wolf dog along, he better be leading him on a string or they both stand a chance of getting shot.

He had his moccasins broke in, and his long hair bunched up and tied with a string under the cowhide cap, and my good two-edged throwing and hunting knife tucked up against his bosom under his shirt. His whiskers was about an inch and a half long, and had started out yella but had turned sort of brindle brown. He didn't really look wild yet, but give his hair and whiskers a few more weeks.

He knowed exactly what he was going to do, and how he was going to do it, if it took him the rest of his life. From my place, he hoofed it towards the blowhole, taking his time, learning the dog to walk one step behind him, and set down whenever Ownie stopped. He didn't have no impatience in him, not a grain of it, nothing but the good feeling a man has when finely he starts a job he has put off too long.

He was headed for Denver, because that was where everybody holed up for the winter when they was broke and hungry or on the dodge. Others might figger the trail of them murderers would lead to the Texas river bottoms, or to the Barbary Coast, or the Superstitions, or someplace like that. But Ownie had it figgered that these was two-bit skunks that'd be scared to death amongst the badmen of the Pecos for instance, or any place it took any guts.

He hoofed it clear to the blowhole, and looked that ugly old place over, because it was his starting place, and that's the way his mind worked, you started at your starting place. It had been a dry autumn, and that dirty old sand was about as ugly as it could be, and the wind was chasing some clouds across the sky, and flapping the tail of his dirty old jacket.

Ownie walked out into that sand a piece. He stood there listening to the fine sand blowing against his pants legs, like he was listening for voices. There wasn't nothing else to blow there but sand, not a leaf or a limb or a piece of trash, and the wind didn't make no sound at all. Just that hissing sand on his pants legs.

Then he seen Charley Polk, the Indian that saved Liddie's life, standing over there in the cactus beside the blowhole, watching him. Ownie walked over to him, and they nodded friends. Charley was standing in the ashes of an old brush camp that Abe Whipple had burned out some time ago, leaving nothing of value even to an Indian.

"Hi, where you going? Where's your horse?" Charley said.

"I sold my horse," Ownie said. "I'm through with the cow business. I'm going to Denver and get a job."

Charley wasn't no fool. He looked them moccasins over, and that long hair and whiskers, and that wolf dog, and said, "Bullshit. You're going to kill them men that kill the old man and little girl."

"Don't you ever say anything like that to nobody," Ownie said. "I don't mess around in your business, don't you mess around in mine."

"Sure, sure," Charley said. "I show you where one of them is, all right?"

"One of them killers?" Ownie said.

"Sure, you come with me," Charley said.

They walked half the day, and then first they come to a horse that had been dead quite a while. The coyotes and buzzards had worked it over pretty good, so Ownie couldn't make out a brand on it, but it had once been a sorrel horse. Its right foreleg was busted all to pieces, coffin and cannon and splint.

Ownie nodded yes, and Charley nodded back, and they both figgered it the same way. Somebody had rode this poor old tired half-dead bonebag as hard as he could be rode in that blizzard, until it put its foot down wrong on some ice under deep snow, and the whole leg caved in.

Charley led him over a little hump in the ground about fifty feet, to where there was the bones of a man. The coyotes and buzzards had been here too, but it was clear the man had been shot in the head, from up high and behind, just blowing his head to pieces.

"I see this man two-three times," Charley said. "He's always got this thing around his neck."

He made motions like a man playing the guitar, but he hadn't ever seen the man close enough to tell what he looked like. You can pick out a sorrel horse and a guitar from a fur piece off.

They looked around for the guitar, but it wasn't nowhere to be seen naturally. They stood there beside them bones for a while, thinking about it, and then Ownie said, "He was afoot in the blizzard, and none of them other three was about to ride double with him."

"Sure, sure," Charley said.

"I can just see it now!" Ownie said. "The more the sonsabitches sobered up, the more they knowed what a terrible mess they was in, lynching was too good for them, and here one of them's horses busts its leg."

"Sure, sure," Charley said.

"They didn't just ride off and leave him. He must of made them some trouble," Ownie said. "So one of them leaned out of the saddle and blowed his head off, and then somebody said, 'Bring along that guitar, it's worth a dollar or two somewheres.' I wonder which way they went!"

"A kid up there on the tracks got a guitar," Charley said.

Ownie thanked him for his help, and they nodded friends to each other again, and then Ownie began walking toward the C.B.&Q. tracks northwest where Charley had pointed, and Charley went back on his own private business whatever it was.

It wasn't long before dark fell. Ownie made a little camp beside a crick, and V.G. started a deer in the brush and high grass, and brought it down close enough to Ownie for him to get to it.

He built his fire bigger, and built a greenwood rack over it, and sliced up a lot of that meat and started to smoke it. It was getting mighty chilly at night by then, but he didn't feel the cold, and he didn't get sleepy or lonesome, and there wasn't no mosquitoes to devil him.

Except when he had to get up to feed the fire, he set there with his knees hunched up with his arms around them, thinking about various things, mostly that he was on the right track. The proof of it was, he had already found one of them. He felt bad that this one had died before he could look him in the eye and make him scream, but there was still three left.

Pretty soon, Liddie Swiverton come to him in the dark, the last thing in the world he expected, because all day when he tried to imagine what she looked like, he just couldn't see nothing.

Now she was just as plain as if she stood there. She wasn't looking at him, but just kind of over his shoulder, and she was smiling, but she didn't like it that he had hung around her just for to find out if she could remember anything that would be useful on the vengeance trail. But he thought maybe she was glad he had reformed, and was off the tanglefoot and the fighting and so forth.

"I have to be honest with you, Liddie," he said. "I only reformed to save money. I don't want to have to stop and work someplace if the trail gets hot."

She didn't answer him back, but by and by another idee come to him, that she would be happy if he would only stop blaming everything on his mother. How did he know the troubles she had? Why should he take the word of people he despised, the way he despised them that took him in after she died. That he had run off from because he hated them so bad?

Liddie Swiverton was the living proof of what Liz Saymill said, that no matter how fur down you started, you could go as high as you aimed if you walked a straight path and kept at it. Ownie always thought of himself about as low as a person could be, the son of a steamboat whore, but the movers was lower still, and a thousand miles below them was the blowholers.

"All right," he said to her, "I won't blame my mother no more. Say, it's mighty peaceful here, Liddie, with just you and me and V.G., ain't it?"

Before Father Lavrens got killed, he used to dearly love to set down with a sipping drink to work on, and tell about them old saints, and what he called their extasy, although it was more like a fit than anything else. They'd take a fit and go off into the desert, or hole up in a cave, and one of them even shinnied up a flagpole and set there the rest of his life, all so they could see God.

They was an all-fired curious people, them saints, and it's a good thing extasy has vanished from the race, because a thing like that could get you arrested these days. But it must of been something like the fit Ownie had, setting there shivering by his fire, and talking to a girl that wasn't there, and making promises and so on. There ain't a whole lot of difference between holy and crazy a good part of the time.

V.G. woke him up at crack of daylight, and he put his smoked meat in his various pockets, and rolled up his blanket, and hiked on. About noon he reached the Q tracks, and in another hour he come to the section house, and there was a whole bunch of kids teasing their pet billy goat under some old runty trees, and one of them had a guitar.

He was trying to play it and couldn't. Ownie was good at anything with his hands, and somewhere on his travels he had learned to chord the guitar, and change keys, and run back and forth and up and down all over the strings, although he couldn't read music. Ownie stopped to ask where he got the guitar, only before the kid could answer, a woman come to the door of the section house with a .410 shotgun.

"Help yourself to a drink at the pump if you like," she said, "and then be off down the track, stranger."

"I'd take a drink kindly, ma'am," Ownie said, "but the reason I stopped, my guitar was stole from me last week, but I see this ain't the one."

"It sure ain't," she said. "My husband bought this'n for the kids way last winter."

"I sure do miss my guitar!" Ownie said. "I wonder if I could try it out a little."

"You might want to buy it," the woman said. "Tommy ain't never going to learn, and it's in good shape."

Ownie took the guitar, and tuned it up, and tried to get limbered up on a few chords. "Oh my you surely can play that thing!" the woman said. "I wonder if you'd play my favorite, 'Neeterwaneeter.'"

"I don't reckon I know that one, ma'am," he said. "Let me see what I can think of."

He fooled around some more, and suddenly she said, "Why say, I thought you told me you didn't know 'Neeterwaneeter'!"

"Oh, that one," Ownie said, and he lined out a few more chords and started to sing. He didn't have no voice like Scotty Dundy, nothing like that, but it was a nice true voice, and maybe better than Scotty on a low grumbly song like this one:

Soft o'er the fountain
Ling'ring falls a southron moon,
While high o'er the mountain
Breaks the dawn too soon.

In thy dark eyes splendor,
Where the loving longing well,
Tearful looks but tender
Brim a fond farewell.
'Nita, Juanita, ask thyself if we must part!
'Nita, Juanita, never leave my heart.

The woman just cried. She said wait till the crew got in and see her husband about buying the guitar. Ownie took their bucksaw and ax and cut up some old ties for firewood for them, and dug the last of their potatoes, and when the crew got in that night, he gave them one dollar for the guitar. The section boss was sure down on cowboys, and even worse on mountain men, and he couldn't remember anything about what the three men looked like.

"Just saddle bums," he said. "Put them on the ground on their feet, and there wasn't a day's work in the three of them. They kept laughing and joking, though, about how this fella Capistrano wasn't going to need his guitar no more."

So it was Capistrano that was dead back there by the blowhole, and had to be scratched off the list. Ownie thanked the man, and said no, he wasn't used to eating at the table and wouldn't have supper with them, and he hiked off down the track with the guitar slung over his shoulder along with his blanket, and V.G. mooching along one step behind. And I reckon when that section boss seen him go off towards the sunset like that, he thought to himself, Good riddance of riffraff.

CHAPTER 10

Winnie Rust had an eight-and-a-half-pound baby girl and they named it Catherine, the closest they could come to Cal for its grandfather, Cal Venaman, who had all the money in the family, and most of what was in the county. "Wouldn't you know that trifling son-in-law of mine would beget a girl!" Cal said. "He can't do anything right."

"You only throwed fillies yourself, Cal," Abe said.

"You've got a point there," Cal admitted, "but let's see what my other son-in-law yields. I don't see how a preacher can be much good at stud, but there are preachers' sons, so perhaps I'm too critical."

"You are, but it's nice to hear you admit it," Abe said.

A while later, Sammie birthed an eight-pound boy, just about all by herself. Rolf was out on his pastoral chores, helping some old sorehead ingrate woman pray some of the meanness out of her before she died, when the pains come on Sammie. She had bread in the oven and a clutch of duck eggs hatching so they could have winter duckling, and she just about waited too long to send for help.

"A fine big handsome boy!" Cal said when he seen his grandson that evening. "What are you going to name him?"

"Martin Luther Ledger," Rolf said.

"For God's sake why?" Cal said.

"That's it, for God's sake," Rolf said. "Martin Luther was a hero of his times, and in this day and age we can use heroism. Maybe some of it will come out on him."

"They'll call him Marty," Cal warned.

"Not in my house, they won't," Rolf said.

"What's the matter with Calvin?" Cal said. "He's the nearest I'll ever come to a son and heir, and I can understand not calling him Rolf, that's an atrocity to put on a helpless baby, but why not stick to a family name?"

The real reason Rolf didn't want to have him named Calvin was because it would be too hard on Thad Rust, and he figgered Thad needed Cal's goodwill worse than he did. They jawed around about it some, Cal holding out for Calvin Martin or Calvin Luther, until Samantha said it was going to be named James Cooper after her grandfather, Opal's father.

James Cooper had come to Wyoming two jumps ahead of an Indiana warrant for shooting a cook in a restaurant that used a woman's name loosely in public. He was too late to get a job with the cattlemen in the range wars, so he organized the nesters into an army, and whipped the hell out of the cattlemen, and then he run for sheriff and had his army keep the cattlemen's crews from voting.

James Cooper was one of the heroes of Wyoming, but not of Indiana, where he had left a wife and three children. He got married again in Wyoming, first to an army colonel's wife, after him and the colonel shot it out, and the colonel took a bad chest wound and retired from the Army. James Cooper then married Opal's mother, who owned the Virginia Dare saloon in Cheyenne, and settled him down.

James Cooper was fifty-four when he married her, and about ready to settle down anyway. His nickname was Stony, something it was pretty hard to explain to women, because it was really short for Old Stone-Ache, since that man had the most ravenous appetite for women in his youth you ever seen. He got gored to death by a bull in his seventy-fourth year, and they half-staffed the flags all over Wyoming.

Cal almost had apoplexy to have his first grandson named after James Cooper, also knowed as Stony Cooper, but he got over it. "He'll have to go to Europe for a wife, to play it safe," Cal said, "because God alone knows how much of Stony's blood and seed are scattered over the nation. A most prodigious breeder, and this boy could grow up to marry his own aunt without knowing it."

Yes, life was going on in Mooney with or without Ownie Cope, as the saying goes. Hoot Swiverton come up for trial, and Cal and his whole crew took the day off to escort the prisoner to the courthouse, and Charley Parker and his whole crew escorted the chief witness, Scotty Dundy. Abe made them all shuck their guns in his office, in a barrel he kept there for that purpose, and warned them that no matter who started a fight in this county, he was always the onc that finished it.

Jimmy Drummond moved to waive a jury, and Miles James objected, because he wanted to lead a cavalry charge past a jury, and fire off his oratorical cannons, and sob into his handkerchief when he pictured Scotty Dundy laying there foully shot down from behind.

"It was from the side, not from behind," Andy said. "This is a simple case and I don't see no reason for taking honest people away from their work and making the county pay jury fees for nothing. So go on with your case, Mr. James, if you please."

Miles made his opening statement, that he was going to prove malice and intent, and then he put Scotty Dundy on the stand. This was Scotty's chance to preen. He said it was the third time he'd been shot but the first time with a rifle, and it was the worst wound he'd ever had because some of the goods of his pants leg went into his meat with the bullet, and stayed there when the bullet went on through.

"It festered up on me," he said, "and I lost three weeks flat on my back in bed, and then was no more than half a man for three weeks after that. So I'm out nearly thirty dollars in pay, besides look how I suffered."

"Do you bear any ill will against the prisoner?" Miles asked him.

Scotty said heavens no, he only pitied the boy and hoped he'd mend his ways before he ended up on the junk heap of life, and he almost got to crying, and he said his own brother had got shipped to Australia for breaking the Queen's peace, and this was what could come of a misspent youth.

Cal Venaman stood up and asked if Scotty meant to say that Charley Parker hadn't paid him while he was laid up, and Charley stood up and said that wasn't the point at all, the point was here was this decent upright cowboy, a visitor in the United States, entitled to all the courtesies of decent human intercourse, and here some of the best blood of Scotland had been spilled.

"Well I'll tell you something, Charley," Cal said. "You must have run those cows I bought from you all the way from your place, the shape they were in. I estimate that they lost ten pounds each between the time I agreed to buy them at your place, and their delivery.

"That's five thousand pounds of beef, two tons and a half. It may not be the best blood of Scotland but it's money out of my pocket. Nevertheless here's what I'll do, I'll pay Scotty fifty dollars out of my own pocket for his lost wages and his pain and suffering, because I know he'll play hell ever getting a dime out of you, a man that would sell another man cattle and then run them to death."

Scotty hit the table with his fist and said, "By God you're a gentleman, Mr. Venaman, nothing like Charley said you were, I'll take it."

"There's one thing I want from you," Cal said.

"I'm at your service, sir," Scotty said.

"I want you to come to the church to sing at the babtism of my grandchildren," Cal said.

Scotty hit the table again and said, "Done, by God! I know all the old Covenanter psalms, and the Church of England liturgy, may God have mercy on me for that, and a bit of Bach that had words set to it—aye, and parts of that one I can whistle like a flute, sir, fit to split your ears. Ye can't beat well-whistled Bach for an infant babtism, sir."

"We have got lost in a box canyon with the brush afire, I'm afraid," Judge Andy Obers said. "Back to the business at hand. I find the prisoner guilty of simple assault and I sentence him to one year in prison. I suspend that sentence and release him to the custody of Cal Venaman for a probation period of five years."

Rolf Ledger said he had scruples about infant babtism, he didn't think it meant a thing except as evidence of the parents' commitment, which shouldn't of been in doubt anyway. He didn't know about whistling in church either, but Cal was in a mood to carry obstacles like a good catch dog chasing a runaway hog, and he had his way.

It turned out to be a real good babtism, with the church packed, and neither baby cried, at least not very much, and Charley Parker gave the little girl a sterling silver napkin ring and the little boy a sterling silver belt buckle. Cal winced a little when Rolf sang out the little boy's name, James Cooper Ledger, and after that he never would call the kid anything but Little Stony.

After the service was over, and before Rolf could break away to get to Cal's buggy to go out to the ranch for dinner, Liddie Swiverton come up to him and asked if she could talk to him a minute. She was still kind of timid, although not rat-scared the way she used to be, and Rolf knowed it took a lot of nerve for her to do it.

"Sure you can, Liddie," he said. "I hope nothing is troubling you, but you know we'll do anything we can."

"Everything's just fine," Liddie said. "I—I only wondered if you had had a letter from Ownie, or anything."

"Why no, I ain't," Rolf said. "Have you?"

"No, Reverend," Liddie said.

He seen how she was suffering, poor girl. He took her by the arm and said, "Liddie, Ownie ain't going to be much of a man to write, I'm afraid. I wouldn't go around asking too many people if they heard from him."

"I won't," she said, about to cry.

He thought to himself, Poor girl, poor innocent, she's the kind that can give her heart but once. He said, "If it will be any comfort to you, I feel this and I feel it pretty strong, Liddie. Whatever Ownie is doing, or wherever he is, he's true to what he believes. No one could ever call Ownie Cope a hypocrite."

That just made her eyes shine. The only trouble was what Ownie was doing, Rolf thought afterward. You can be sincere as hell about the wrong things.

CHAPTER 11

It was getting cold by the time Ownie got to Denver, and his moccasins was broke in, and his hair and whiskers had made their crop. Like in every railroad division point, there was a place where men passing through could jungle up, and there was more than usual of them in Denver, because there wasn't a job in five hundred miles once winter had set in.

Ownie come padding in on his moccasins, with his blanket and guitar slung over his back, and V.G. stealing along at his heels, and he looked just like a mountain man who couldn't own up that his day was long over. There was several camps in this brush near the Q yards. He could of joined any of them, but he went off and built his own fire, and ate some of his smoked meat, and then got his guitar out and played and sang a couple of lonesome old songs.

Men from other camps come over to listen. Ownie didn't pay them no mind, and they knowed better than to try to socialize with a mountain man. When he left off singing, they went back to their own camps, and talked about what a wild mean ornery bunch them mountain men was.

Ownie set there until Liddie come to him through the dark, when his fit of extasy got strong enough. He called her honey but he didn't mean nothing by it, it was the same as he'd call a little child that. He said, "Honey, I'm a-getting there. Your pap and your sister can rest in peace before I'm through."

He rolled up in his blanket and slept, safe as in a church with V.G. beside him. In the morning, he put his blanket and guitar on his back and walked into Denver. The police knowed about these mountain men and left him alone. He was looking for where men hung out to find jobs, because that was how he expected to get onto these other three blowholers.

He went past a store with a sign, S. H. Bosch, Locksmith, and on a hunch went in. S. H. Bosch was Blind Bosch, the best blind locksmith in the business. He said he was always looking for a good hand, but being blind, it had to be somebody he could trust, and did Ownie have any references.

"No, and there's no reason you should trust me," Ownie said. "Nobody else ever did to speak of."

"Is that your dog with you?" Blind Bosch said.

Ownie said it was, and Blind asked him what kind of dog it was, and Ownie said quarter-strain wolf, and Bosch said well if his dog trusted him, he guessed he could. Ownie went to work there, and while it was a long time since he had been in a lockshop, he hadn't forgot much of it and he was always good with his hands.

He went back to the jungle every night to cook himself a little supper, and play his guitar, and go into his fit of extasy with Liddie. One night, when he put the guitar away and started to roll up in his blanket, one of them men that had been listening to him said, "Pardner, you sure can play that guitar."

Ownie acted like he didn't hear him, but he looked this man over pretty good. He was God knew how old, anywhere from thirty to sixty, you couldn't tell because he had drank enough tanglefoot to raise the Platte a foot. He looked like he had the consumption, and his old snag teeth couldn't chew nothing tougher than chicken, but you bet he thought he was some kind of a cowboy. He had the boots and the hat all right.

But there was no rope calluses on his hands, and no stirrup chafes on his boots, and this is how you can tell if a man has been working cows lately. Ownie wondered if he was getting a hunch about this fella, but he just laid down in his blanket and let V.G. snuggle up to him.

The man wouldn't go away. "I wonder if I could ask you where you got that guitar," he said.

"You can ask," Ownie said.

"I will then, where'd you get it?" the man said.

"Do you say it ain't mine?" Ownie said, and set up. "Who are you to be saying it ain't my guitar?"

He chunked a piece of wood on the fire to brighten it up, and he give this old bum a mountain-man stare, and this old bum said, "Bristol's the name, Hart Bristol, why good God, nothing is farther from my mind. It just looked like one that used to belong to a friend of mine."

"Well it ain't," Ownie said. "I bought it from a Q section boss less than a month ago."

This Hart Bristol give a kind of a lurch and a sigh, and he

got up and excused himself and went over and set down at the next fire. Ownie whispered to himself, "So your name is Hart Bristol, well that's a good start, I wonder which one you are? Not the gunfighter sure as hell. Mr. Bristol, your days is numbered, you son of a bitch."

He had the guitar wrapped up in a length of dry goods, and just for meanness he unwrapped it again and set down to play and sing. He knowed it had hit Bristol hard when he said he had bought it from the Q section boss, well let him set there and listen to it a while longer.

The next night Bristol was back; it was just like he was haunted by that guitar, he just *had* to come stumbling over every time he heard Ownie hit it a lick. This went on for quite a few nights.

Then another old mountain man showed up, and come like a bee to Ownie's fire, a real old-timer gone loony like all of them old ones is. Ownie let him sleep there. His name was Pat Edgerton, and he knowed about a gray stallion that had been stole by the Indians in the Uintahs, and had got away from them and went wild. The Mormons would pay five thousand dollars to get that horse back.

The next morning he started talking about that gray stallion again, so Ownie run him away, and Pat Edgerton went over to another camp and began talking about it, and Ownie packed up his camp and left. He told Blind Bosch he would be gone awhile, and might not be back at all, and Blind said, "I expected it, and it's too bad because you have the touch. I'll prove it to you. Here, see if you can pick this lock."

He handed Ownie a lock, and Ownie fiddled around with it awhile, with some wires and the blade of his knife and an awl and some stiff paper, and in a minute he popped it open. Blind said, "There you are, that's one of the best locks on the market, nobody has ever picked it in less than ten minutes before."

"Why did you do that?" Ownie said.

"To give you something to think about, mountain man," Blind said. "You could be a good house robber or a good locksmith, either one. Think about that."

"I may be back," Ownie said.

He bought a chunk of beef and took it back out to his camp. He took out my two-edged hunting knife and stropped it on his moccasin like a mountain man, and then sliced this beef up and began smoking it. Soon as he set down to unwrap his guitar, Hart Bristol come over and made himself to home beside the fire.

"I bet you're heading for the Uintahs," he said.

Ownie plumb ignored him. In a minute, Bristol said, "That crazy old bastard wanted a pardner to help catch that gray horse, but I wouldn't fool around with an old fool like him. I'd go pardners with you though."

"There ain't no gray horse," Ownie said.

"Yes there is, I've heard about him before," Bristol said.

"It's just a lot of talk," Ownie said, and it was, because he'd heard about the Gray Ghost as far back as Little Rock, when he was only thirteen years old. Maybe there was such a horse once, but he'd of been thirty years old by now, and anyway if the Mormons couldn't catch him, nobody could.

"If it's just a lot of talk," Bristol said, "where are you fixing to go?"

It took Ownie until almost noon the next day to smoke his meat, and when he packed it up and throwed his guitar and blanket on his back, here come Hart Bristol again.

"Take me with you," he said. "I want to go pardners with you."

"If I wanted a pardner it wouldn't be you," Ownie said. "What good would you be to anybody?"

"I used to break horses for outfits in Nebraska and Dakota," Bristol said. "I been in a streak of bad luck, but it's time it changed, and if it turns good for me, it'll turn good for you too. Your luck always hits bottom sometime and starts back up, don't it?"

Ownie never did admit he was going after the gray horse. It seemed to him that his pitiful hangdog admirer, Hart Bristol, was just purely bewitched by that guitar. That guitar started me on my downfall, Bristol was saying to himself, and now it's my charm to change my luck back.

Ownie didn't know how he knowed this, but he did, so sure in his soul it was another fit of extasy in him. A hunch is one thing, anybody can have a hunch, but a fit of extasy is different. It's like drawing aces back to back, and waiting for the third one, and it drops on the fifth card, and you just *know* the other man is setting there with a king buried to match the pair showing.

"I'm going," Ownie said. "I can't help if you go along, you old fool."

He just walked Bristol's hind end off. In a week or ten days, Bristol was toughened to it a little better, and being shut off from the whisky, he healthed up whether he wanted to or not. But by then they was high up in the Rockies, right where Ownie wanted them to be. Ownie led Bristol all over, back and forth and up and down.

It wasn't distance he wanted, it was for Bristol to blab something. Bristol wasn't no walking man, but he was sure a talking man. Something was eating at his mind, and he couldn't fetch it out and he couldn't leave it lay there. He was too tired to talk until Ownie fed him, but the minute Ownie got the guitar out, Bristol started talking. He didn't talk about anything in particular. He just rambled, everything from how his family had to eat acorns when the Yanks burned them out when he was a kid, to an old sow that had sixty-six pigs for them in four years, two litters a year.

Not once did Liddie come to see Ownie in a fit of extasy. Bristol just talked her away.

They was up about eight thousand feet the afternoon the fog come in on them. One minute, it was bright and clear around them and the clouds was sliding along overhead, the next, they couldn't see each other ten feet away. The wind was just like ice, not very strong, but it drilled in.

"Have to camp," Ownie said, because a mountain man never said no more than he had to.

"Let's try to get back down below it," Bristol kind of whimpered. "I ain't skeered of lightning or anything else, but I'm superstitious about fog. We could make us a torch out of something."

Ownie just grunted. Bristol felt around until he found some brush, and he got his knife out and cut a torch, and he borried Ownie's flint and steel and somehow got it to burning. But all it done was blind both of them.

"A-a-a-ah hell, no good, no good!" Bristol said. His teeth began to chatter. "Let's make a fire. Fog just drives me crazy! How about a fire?"

Ownie just grunted. Bristol felt around until he found a little old bush growing. He couldn't get Ownie to help him cut it, and he couldn't put the torch down to cut it himself, and he just had to set fire to it where it growed. It didn't burn very good or last very long, and then it was dark again, and all he could do was try to find Ownie in the dark, and set there shivering beside him like a kid that's scared of the dark.

Ownie retch over and unwrapped his guitar, and Bristol said, "God, man, don't play tonight, not in this fog, man, come on!"

Ownie just grunted. Bristol felt around for some more brush and couldn't find any. He couldn't see anything, but he knowed Ownie was still holding the guitar.

"I ask you man to man, don't play it," Bristol said.

Ownie just grunted and fixed his fingers the way he wanted them on the frets, and he drawed his right thumbnail across the strings real slow, *tim, tam, tom, tum, toom!* Bristol let out a bleat and catched hold of his arm.

"I asked you man to man not to!" he said.

Ownie hooked a fingernail under one string and give it a good tug and let go, and quivered his left finger on the fret, and it went *toom-m-m, woom-woom-woom-m-m, wah-wah-toom-m-m-m-m* until it died out. And he thought, Here is where we come out of the chute a-bucking.

"Did you ever commit a terrible crime?" Bristol said. "I tell you nobody knows how it can haunt you, and you get into it drunker than a skunk, a thing you wouldn't do in a thousand years sober. The man that owned that guitar, he was the son of a bitch that got me into it."

Ownie just grunted. Bristol said, "Listen, I'll tell you about it, and you tell me who's to blame. *He* wasn't drunk, you bet your boots on that, he was stone sober, the son of a bitch. He leaned that guitar up against a rock and said, 'Let's go down and jolly them girls around a little, and warm our shanks.' And by God picked it up again afterward without even wiping that old man's blood off'n his hands."

It just poured out. The man with the guitar was Capistrano Erland, born in San Juan Capistrano, and a sailor by trade until he got tired of it. Bristol and Capistrano met on a haying crew near Grand Island, Nebraska, the B Bar B. When they got laid off come fall, they decided to go to Denver because it was a good town to be out of work in.

They got as far as Mooney before winter set in, and there they bought a pint to warm up on, and the next thing they knowed they was broke, and Sheriff Abe Whipple was giving all of them two and a half minutes to get out of town. He didn't know any of the others but Capistrano Erland, but the others turned out to be Jimmy Rackstraw and Doc Harper. They had got friendly somehow on his and Capistrano's whisky.

They all ended up out at the blowhole. Ownie almost let out a yell when he heard them other two names. He knowed Jimmy Rackstraw himself, from when they both worked for a while on the Roofed Lazy 8. He could barely remember him, but he knowed the name.

Doc Harper's name was well advertised among them that kept up with the legends of the speed-gun artists. Doc had the name of being one of the best. Ownie hadn't heard about him being in the pen, but that's where he went, for killing a man in Wichita.

These four holed up out there at the blowhole, four prime specimens of the blowholer, drifters blowed together by an ill wind as the saying goes. Doc had an idee for making some money, and they had to have money or starve. It was a long cold ride to Denver on an empty gut.

"Doc said he knowed a preacher in Mooney that had been a convict himself," Bristol said. "He said he hit this preacher up for a stake, and was turned down just because he'd been liquoring up a little, and the son of a bitch just dripped fat like a goose, he was so rich. He said the four of us could pull it off easy, and hold him until his father-in-law come up with ten thousand dollars."

Nobody would of took any such fool plan serious except a bunch of saddle bums, especially if they knowed how hard it was to pry a dime out of Cal Venaman. The plan was to ride to my place and shoot me through the window, because Doc said I was a no-good son of a bitch, anyway.

Capistrano would ride into Mooney, him being the cleanest one, and tell Rolf that Doc Harper was dying out at my place, and wanted to make his peace with God. That would fetch Rolf out if anything would.

It was only too bad they didn't keep their minds on their business, because killing me has been tried, and nobody gets past my dogs. I been an outlaw myself, and I know who to trust, and so do my dogs. I would of learned them a lesson about who to fool around with, and them Swiverton murders wouldn't of happened.

But on their way to my place, they seen this mover's camp and decided to jolly the girls around. Bristol remembered every little thing that happened.

Capistrano drawed a blank at first, because the girl he chased pulled him off'n his horse and got away, and he had to come back and take leavings. Bristol and Harper and Rackstraw all had a shot at the old pap, and it was Rackstraw that quirted Hoot.

All four of them helped kill Alice. Bristol said he couldn't forget, it was so awful. "I can't describe it," he said, "and you couldn't believe it unless you seen her."

Ownie said, "I did see her, you son of a bitch, what do you think I've got you up here all to myself for?"

It was a mistake to blurt it out like that with the guitar still on his lap, but he couldn't help it. Bristol had some hair-trigger nerves himself, and they told him right now that he had picked the wrong man to ease his conscience with, and what to do about it.

Bristol kicked out and catched Ownie in the mouth with the

heel of his boot, and Ownie rolled back and pulled my good two-edged knife out, and he heard the *whk-k-kng* of Bristol getting his own knife out, and he thought what a hell of an avenger he was to get caught like this.

If he was as good as dead, he might as well take his chances, so he come up hitting and slashing, and once their knives clashed and he seen sparks. It was just spooky, them two knife-fighting up there in the fog in the night, but he seen that he had the best knife anyway. Bristol cut his coat a little for him before Ownie made a lucky grab and catched his knife arm by the wrist.

He started to bend it back, and now he could laugh right in Bristol's face because he had the strength over Bristol. He said, "You son of a bitch, I ain't going to kill you yet, I'll see you live a long, long time, hurting every minute of it. But start thinking about it now why don't you, because I know tricks an Indian wouldn't of used."

Bristol give a big jumping jerk and began to scream, but it wasn't a fit, it was old V.G. that come up at him without a sound, purely like a wolf. Ownie couldn't see a thing but shadows as Bristol jerked loose from him, and at more than four feet, not even shadows.

Bristol catched hold of Ownie's leg, and Ownie felt himself sliding. He kicked the leg as hard as he could as fast as he could, and he shook Bristol off, and he managed to stop sliding.

But Bristol didn't. He just kept sliding and sliding and screaming and screaming, and then there was one last blood-curdler that thinned out fast as he stopped sliding and fell free, and then it was cut off short when he hit somewhere a long way down. A real long way.

Ownie thought he had lost them both into a Rocky Mountain gorge, Bristol and his dog as well, but then V.G. come scrambling up the slope on his belly, clawing like he was digging out a badger, and he got up to where it was safe. Ownie laid there quite a while, and then he began squirming up one little squirm at a time, prob'ly half an hour to climb the length of his body.

But she leveled out under him at last, and V.G. was licking his face, and he could get up on his knees and crawl after the dog to where he had left his blanket and guitar. He just rolled up in the blanket and laid there and shivered, with the dog right next to him.

Well that is two that got away from me, he thought to himself, but I ain't going to complain about my luck, not after making it back up here.

It was noon the next day before the fog cleared. Him and Bristol had been stopped in about the worst place they could of picked. Down below there was nothing but an ocean of fog with the sun shining on it, and the trail wasn't more than five or six feet wide, and then this sharp short slope, and then nothing.

He took it slow going down. He had to camp on the trail another night when the fog closed in, but the next morning it cleared up nice and bright and cold and windy. He let V.G. pick the way, mostly by smelling the tracks they'd made coming up. Finely they reached the bottom.

Ownie's coat was just slashed to pieces, and V.G. had a cut on his ribs.

But Ownie could look back and see the eagles and hawks and buzzards starting to spiral down, now that the fog had cleared out. Hart Bristol had fell about five hundred feet, and then had hit a rock outcrop, and then bounced another two hundred feet before landing in a tree.

There he hung, head down, waiting for the birds to pick him. "A quicker death than you deserve," Ownie said to him. "That's two of you got away from me. Well better luck next time."

CHAPTER 12

Heading back to Denver, Ownie didn't feel so good and he didn't know why, but he didn't seem to have no strength, and he couldn't sleep well at night nor wake up easy in the morning. He passed by a place where a man was running cattle in a nice little mountain valley, and the winter had held off, and he was getting in some lucky late hay.

He thought he'd ask for a job, and he done it, and the rancher didn't exactly kill the fatted calf for a worthless no-account mountain man. But after Ownie worked there a couple of days, and the man seen he could and would do the job, he let Ownie take charge of the gang. His name was Jerry Clyde, and his brand was the JC, so of course naturally his place was known far and wide as the Jesus Christ.

Ownie stayed with him almost to Christmas. It was like his mind had went to sleep on him and the rest of him hadn't. He couldn't make up his mind to anything. He felt sheepish and guilty, like he was dodging his duty, and yet it was just the purest kind of pleasure to get out here and make this winter hay, and work his tail off.

Jerry knowed Ownie had something on his mind, and he give him every chance to talk about it, but he wasn't the kind of a man to pry. He let Ownie live in the bunkhouse, but he found a few chances to put him at jobs where he'd have to eat with the family. He had four little kids, three boys and a girl, and he let them hang around whenever Ownie was doing anything safe for kids, like shoeing horses or banking up around the house against winter.

Then finely one night, Liddie come back to Ownie. He hadn't seen her since before Hart Bristol come to his death up there in the mountains. He was out in the barn all night, waiting for a little pony of the kids to throw her colt. It come to him all of a sudden, what if it was him and Liddie had a place like this away to hell and gone by themselves, and kids of their own to raise, and so on.

And there she was. He had never seen her clearer, not even when they was together there in Mooney before he hit the vengeance trail. She was wearing a white waist she made for herself with Miss Liz's help, with a high ruffly collar, and a row of little pearl buttons down the front, and that black Indian hair was pulled back so her ears showed, and held by a little ribbon behind.

He'd only seen her that way once, on her way to church with Liz, when he was blundering around half drunk and had to slide behind a tree quick to keep her from seeing him. She looked so happy going to church, and Miss Liz looked so proud of her.

"Well hello there, Liddie," he said to her there in the barn, and in his vision you might say, she kind of smiled, and he thought for about a second that she was going to look straight at him and say something.

"I just figgered something out, Liddie," he said. "You want to know what it is? I always reckoned what made you so happy in Mooney was that people respected you. They didn't ever respect me, no not a bit, but they did you, and I was so proud of you because of that! You never knowed that, Liddie, but I was. I seen you in the jaws of hell, and I seen you come back, and I seen you just bud out like a rose bush when people respected you.

"But you know what, Liddie, that ain't the main thing, the main thing is you respect *yourself;* you got out of the wagon and you held up your head, and you vowed to live up to what your pap wanted for you. It's more important to respect yourself than to have people respect you, ain't it?

"Something else, Liddie, I disrespected myself all my life because of my mother, and now my eyes is open I'm so ashamed I could go sleep with the hogs, but it ain't going to be like that no more.

"I mean to respect *my*self too, and I hope others come to respect me like they do you, but if they don't I ain't going to blame my mother or my luck or anything, I'm going to take aim on self-respect and let the world go hang if it has to. This is what old Rolf means when he says look into your heart, well I reckon he ain't such a fool as he sounds at times, well I see you're going to fade away on me and my mare is straining to drop her baby, but I sure do appreciate your coming around.

"So long, Liddie, for tonight."

She did fade away all right, and he tussled with the little mare until he seen it was too much for him, and about one-thirty in the morning he went up to the house and stirred Jerry out, and later Jerry went up and got his wife, and the three of them finely got this nice big living he-colt out alive, and made it stand and suck. There just about ain't no nicer feeling than to win that kind of a battle, and see that colt stilting around, he thinks that box stall is his whole world and my ain't it big! But just wait until he can get outside, you think.

They had their breakfast about four-thirty of the morning, and Jerry got to telling him about this other place he had bought about thirty-five miles to the west five years ago, planning for his sister's husband to run it for him. The brother-in-law worked for a feed and seed company in Denver, and wasn't a bit happy, but when he checked out to work for Jerry, he come up eight hundred dollars short in his accounts.

"I made it up for him," Jerry said, "but you can't have a man like that running your place and handling your own money. I been running it myself in a half-ass way, but in mountain country, you either run your property with an iron hand or it goes back to the brush."

"That's true, it does all right," Ownie said. "It goes wilderness, and the bears get your calves, and snow breaks down your fences, and the wild studs steal your saddle horses. Ain't everybody can ranch in mountains."

"You could. It's too bad you ain't a family man, Ownie," Jerry said, "because there's a furnished four-room house there, and a good buggy and team goes with it, and I'd start you with fifty hens and a dozen ducks and a drake. I'd go as high as fifty dollars a month and ten per cent of the increase for the right man."

"I ain't the right man, Jerry," Ownie said. "In fact it's time for me to move on, but I thank you anyhow."

He dickered with Jerry over what was owed him, and rode out of there on a small but real good five-year-old gelding by the name of Bud, with a good saddle, and a nice big heavy sheepskin coat that Jerry had got too fat for.

He was in good shape for money and things, but the main

thing was, he could get on with his job of finding Jimmy Rackstraw and Doc Harper, and killing them. He seen finely what had just about paralyzed him for a while.

He looked into his heart and seen that he'd been just plain scared to death by nearly going over the edge up there with Hart Bristol. Ownie knowed he wasn't a coward, or never had been before anyways. But it took all the nerve in him to face what made him scared of dying now.

Liddie.

Yes, when he started out to ask himself why life was suddenly that dad-blamed important, the answer was Liddie. Once you've drug your badger out of the hole, you can rassle with him, and Ownie knowed he wasn't the man for her, nothing was surer in life than that. Escape the wagons, and then marry the likes of *him?*

Oh no, he thought to himself as he rode on to Denver, my head is clear now, I've got my nerve back, I won't be dreaming no more impossible dreams, so on with the job cowboy. . . .

It had to be Jimmy Rackstraw that talked with a Scotch brogue. It sounded just like him to Ownie. Jimmy was one of them sneaks with a big mouth that's always in trouble, but you never catch him in a fight, he'll ride you as long as you let him, but just call him up short and see what he says.

"Me? Why what're you mad at *me* for? What did *I* ever do to you? Call you names, why *I* wouldn't call *you* no names, can't you take a little *fun?* You ain't got no better friend than me, stop faunching and let's shake hands, no I ain't going to fight you over no such foolishness."

Jimmy had knowed better than to let his big mouth run on about Ownie, in fact Ownie barely remembered him, and wasn't sure he'd know him if he seen him again.

But Jimmy could of picked up the Scotch brogue from Scotty Dundy, and it was the kind of a thing he'd use to make fun of Scotty with, and Scotty too good natured to know he was being insulted. According to Hart Bristol, it was old weak-kneed Jimmy that hung back, and didn't want to rough the girls up at first, only when Alice got to crying and screaming, he—but it was something Ownie didn't want to think about.

But in some ways, Jimmy Rackstraw was the worst of the four.

Just outside of Denver, Ownie met an old cowboy who was so bitter he started hollering before they was fifty yards apart. "You got a gun on under that coat?" he said. "If you have, just kiss yourself good-by."

"Why should I do that?" Ownie said.

"Them Goddamn Denver police, that's why," the old man said. "They got a new rule now, you can't wear a gun, not even a holster, what kind of a law is that? They'll take it away from you and kick you out of town, well they don't have to kick me out, I hope I never see Denver again, with their Goddamn narrow-minded police."

"I don't pack a gun," Ownie said. "Well so long, old-timer, see you at roundup time as the saying goes."

"Not in Denver you won't," the old man said.

Rolf Ledger was always in favor of a law against packing a gun, but Ownie never heard of nobody else doing it, and it kind of surprised him that a law-abiding town like Denver would stoop so low. Not that it meant anything to him, so long as he got his chance to catch Jimmy Rackstraw and torture him to death with my fine two-edged knife.

He got in late in the afternoon, and decided he'd go and see Blind Bosch first, and find out if it was any use coming back to work there. There was a saloon on the corner down the block from Blind Bosch's place, and it had a good hitch rack, so he thought he'd tie his horse Bud up there, and walk to Blind's place.

There was this policeman, Virg Kling, that walked the beat there, and Ownie had got to know him. Virg didn't recognize Ownie when he seen him. He said, "Hold up there, cowboy, before you tie your horse."

"Sure, Virg, what's the trouble?" Ownie said.

Virg said, "Well I'll be damned, the mountain man himself, what are you doing on a horse?"

"I learned to ride," Ownie said. "A man put me up on a little pony and held my hand until I got done crying, try it yourself sometime. What's this foolishness about not wearing a gun, anyway?"

"Open your coat up and let's make sure," Virg said. "If you was my own brother, I'd have to search you. Well all right, you ain't armed, go in peace as the Good Book says. We had four cowboy fights since Saturday night, or wars is a better word. I never seen such quarrelsome people, just for the fun of it. Come winter they're all broke, and then they find whisky somewhere, they can't eat but they can always raise a drink, and then they have to prove what dangerous men they are. The people of Denver are sick and tired of it."

"I can see their point of view," Ownie said, "but I don't drink and I ain't armed, Virg."

Virg went into the saloon on the corner, Danny Burgoon's place, and Ownie tied his horse and started to walk down to see Blind Bosch. He almost got there, when this fella come out of a place with a sign Gents Furnished Rooms, and started for the corner.

Jimmy Rackstraw!

Jimmy wasn't in range clothes except he still wore boots. He had a long brown overcoat, and a wool cap with earflaps, and he was smoking a big cigar. He looked like a town man for sure, but there wasn't no possibility of a mistake, this was Jimmy Rackstraw.

It took Ownie some time to get his wits back, he didn't know how long, but quite a while because when he woke up, Jimmy was just running up the steps of Danny Burgoon's saloon. And Ownie was suddenly shaking all over, the way Jimmy must of shook when them other three said let's go rough up them girls a little, like his nerve had just left him completely.

What kind of an avenger am I anyway, he said to himself. He unbuttoned one button of his coat, and one of his shirt, and made sure he could get at the knife. He went after Jimmy right there in the heart of Denver, but he might as well of been Blind Bosch himself, because at the bottom of Danny

Burgoon's place he bumped into a strange policeman and didn't see him at all.

"Hold it there, my boy, who do you think you're bumping into?" the policeman said.

"Excuse me," Ownie said, "but I'm in a hurry."

"So am I," the policeman said. "Coat button not buttoned and the right hand inside, now that's interesting, let's have a look at your gun, my boy, like a good boy."

"I ain't got no gun," Ownie said.

He thought he was going to faint, but he didn't. The policeman retch in and took the knife, and said, "A knife is it? By God, you're a cool one, but we'll warm the ass of you in jail a few days, how's that my boy?"

I can't do it, Ownie said to himself. At the last moment I'm yellow-bellied, a hell of an avenger, but at least he ain't going to get away, I swear to God that. . . . He said, "Listen, there's a man in the saloon there that's wanted for murder. Ask Virgil Kling. He's in there now. Get Virg out here, he'll believe me, Virg knows me, I tell you that son of a bitch is a wanted murderer in there!"

And all he could feel was thankfulness that it had been took out of his hands this way. The policeman trusted him, although not very far, because he held Ownie and sent a boy into the saloon to bring Virg out.

"What do you mean, a murderer, mountain man?" Virg said. "I know everybody in there, they're regulars, not a murderer among them. What kind of a sandy are you trying to run, mountain man?"

"I can point him out to you," Ownie said.

"You do exactly that," Virg said.

"He'll be armed, too."

"He better not be. You show us."

Ownie stepped up and took a quick peek by opening the door and letting it close. "Him," he said. "The one at the end, with the ear flaps and the cigar."

"Oh hell, that's only Dutch Johnny," Virg said. "They call him that because he can talk like a Dutchman until you'd swear he was one. He don't amount to a hill of beans, he works in the express company stables, but me and Francis Kennedy here knows him well, don't we, Francis?"

The other policeman said, "Not well enough to go his bond, Virgil my boy. Let's hear more of this from the mountain man."

Ownie said, "I swear to God, let me smoke him out, I promise I can do it! He helped kill an old man and a young girl, the filthiest kind of murder, it makes me sick just to think of it. Sheriff Whipple, Mooney County, got out some dodgeroos on it. I'll tell you what you go and do, ask him if he's a Scotchman, get him to talking Scotch!"

"Now wait a minute, Virgil my boy!" Kennedy said. "I've seen the paper he speaks of, a man with a Scotch brogue, and there's a bit of a reward on him I think. Can it hurt to find out?"

"You stay here, mountain man," Virg said.

They talked it over between them, and they made Ownie wait. Virg went back into the saloon and went over to the door of the can and waited there, so he was behind Jimmy Rackstraw. In a minute, Francis Kennedy went in and took off his overcoat, and unbuttoned the flap of his holster on the sly. He walked up to Jimmy.

"A cold day, Johnny boy," he said. "As me kinsmen in Scotland say, a r-r-raw, drear-r-r-ry day wi'out a wee drappie to war-r-rum the bones."

Old silly Jimmy grinned a big silly grin, and his big mouth took charge and led him right down the chute for fools. He said, "Ah, be ye a Scot, man? Aye, 'tis a cold one, vur-r-ra cold, God pity the puir-r-r," and that was all the farther he got.

"Son of a bitch, the mountain man is right," Francis Kennedy said. "Keep your hands in sight, I arrest you on suspicion of murder—*oh no you don't!*"

Jimmy went for his gun, the worst thing he could of done unless he wanted to die. Prob'ly he'd seen them dodgeroos of Abe Whipple's, and knowed his Scotch accent was his trademark of murder, and realized he had shot off his big mouth once too often.

The two policemen was facing each other, with Jimmy

Rackstraw between them, so they had a problem about shooting. Virg Kling dropped down on one knee and fired upward, and he catched Jimmy where the neck meets the left shoulder, and tore out about a pound of his meat. Francis Kennedy shot him close to the crotch, not right in it but close enough to make him a soprano if he lived.

Jimmy never got off a shot. Francis Kennedy took his gun away from him, while Virg went to get an ambulance. The ambulance got there, but then one of the horses slipped on the ice and went down, and they was twenty minutes getting him up. A doctor from down the street plugged up Jimmy's bullet holes, while Ownie stood there and talked to Jimmy about the murder.

Jimmy denied everything. He said he didn't know Hart Bristol or Capistrano Erland or Doc Harper, hadn't never heard of them, hadn't been in Mooney for three years, and hadn't never been in any trouble with the law.

"You're a lying son of a bitch," Ownie said. "You fired one shot into the old man, and you abused that poor girl worse than anybody, and you're the one that plugged Capistrano when he run out of luck and crippled his horse."

"I swear I didn't, Ownie," Jimmy said. "Why are you doing this to me, Ownie? What did I ever do to you, Ownie? You and me was always friends."

"All right, go to the gallus with that lie on your soul on top of everything else," Ownie said.

Jimmy looked at the doctor that was patching him up and said, "Is it bad? Oh how I hurt! Will I live? It ain't fatal, is it? Oh God I hope it ain't fatal."

"You're through at stud," the doctor said, "but you won't die."

All the way to the hospital in the ambulance, Jimmy kept swearing he wasn't no murderer, and so forth, but then they chloroformed him to sew him up, and when he come out of the chloroform he was blabbing away for all he was worth about the murders. There was two nurses helping, and the things he told, one of them nurses had to go out and throw up, and it's pretty hard to make an old-time nurse in a police hospital throw up.

That night Jimmy ripped his bandages off and deliberately bled himself to death. "The double-crossing son of a bitch, he beat us out of five hundred dollars," Virg Kling said. "Look, the bulletin says delivered alive to undersigned, how do you like that?"

"I'm sorry about that," Ownie said, "but I'm glad he died the way he did. Him and them other two, Hart Bristol and Capistrano Erland, have got a lot to talk over now, wherever they are. And I bet I know where."

"What are you going to do now, mountain man?" Virg said.

"Don't call me that. I just fixed up this way to find these bastards, and it worked," Ownie said. "But now I'm going to get my hair cut and a shave, and go home."

"What about the other one, the gunfighter?" Virg said.

Ownie throwed up his hands. "I don't know," he said. "I ain't the man to avenge nobody, that's for positive. I can plan as mean as anybody alive, but at the last minute, somehow I lose heart. Just one other thing, boys. If you come across Doc Harper, don't give him the chance that you give Rackstraw!"

"We didn't give Rackstraw any chance," Francis Kennedy said.

"It was still too much," Ownie said.

CHAPTER 13

There was this show come to town in April, the Ambrose Repertory Company, or ARC Players as they liked to be knowed as, and they wanted to use the Methodist church, and would pay two dollars a night for it. The board said they'd be guided by their pastor, and Rolf talked it over with Madison Monroe Ambrose, and Ambrose said it would only be selected passages from Shakespeare, and they always left out the gamy parts when they played in a church.

Rolf said he wasn't up on Shakespeare, but there was parts of the Old Testament that would curl your hair, Lot's daughters for instance, and Ambrose said, "Right you are, Parson, we see eye to eye, nothing that will offend the Methodist conscience will be presented, not even the death of Desdemona, and there goes one of our best ones right out the window."

Madison Monroe Ambrose was sixty-eight years old then, and it took a quart a day just to keep steam up in his boilers, but he hardly ever showed he'd took a drink. He was a mighty spry man, quick-minded and a good talker, and he'd been all over the world. He said he had never played before the Queen, but he had entertained her soldiers in Egypt, India, and the Bahamian Islands, and he'd met the Empress Eugénie when times was better for both him and the Empress, and he'd met three Spanish-American presidents, one of which still survived. Me and him got to be pretty good friends. He paid cash for his drink and never made a scene, and that's a good enough recommendation for anybody.

Paying cash for his whisky might of been one reason the ARC Players went broke in Mooney, and had to stay there until they earned their fare out of town; anyway they was still there when Ownie Cope finely come back. He come to my place first, about daybreak.

"I'll take my gun back now, Pete," was the first thing he said to me.

He handed over my knife, and I looked it over and seen it was in good shape, and I said, "I reckon there's no use asking for my dog back, he'll be your dog now."

Ownie said, "I'd miss him and he'd miss me. I wish I could work out a deal on him that I could afford."

"Go ahead and keep him," I said. "Nothing makes you less profit than trying to keep a dog that don't want to stay. I reckon you'll want to turn in now, if you've rode all night."

"No, I camped at the blowhole," Ownie said. "That place has sure become disinhabited. It don't look like nobody has camped there for a long time."

"Abe or Thad rides out there every time they're in the neighborhood, and they've had to wet down a couple of fires and kick a couple of rumps," I said, "but the blowhole has got a bad reputation, and is knowed far and wide as a good place to miss."

"There was shells in this gun when I left it with you," Ownie said. I give him some shells, and he loaded up the gun and buckled on the holster, and said, "It's sure a lonesome old place to camp. You could just about believe in ghosts there, Pete. You can just about hear ghostly footsteps."

He got off on a long story he'd heard, about a man down in Honduras who owned the worst old sandy blowhole anywhere, that he'd heard about in Denver. They had a scourge of dogs that went wild down there, and they was killing off livestock and even people, and the government put a bounty on them and got just thousands of them killed off.

He said this man that owned the Honduras blowhole, he offered the government his land to bury them dogs in free of charge, and they took him up on it, and he just worked his hind end off for a year, burying them thousands of dogs. Then he just set back a few years, and then planted himself a bananner grove, and that blowhole had become so fertile he became a big rich important bananner king.

He said he didn't see no other solution for the blowhole we had, it had to be made fertile some way, and get a crop started there, and wipe the blight off'n the face of Creation. I said, "We're a mite short on dogs for that, and you'd play hell raising bananners here anyway, but keep thinking, Ownie, you'll come up with something."

"Same old joker," Ownie said. "Sweet clover would fertile up that Goddamn hellhole, if you could get it started. If you sowed it every year, sooner or later you'd get a wet year, and it'd take holt."

I said he was getting warm, it was better than the bananner idee, and I'd back anything that had a ghost of a chance to wipe out the blowhole. He grinned more like his old self, and said he reckoned he'd go on into town.

He was a lot thinner, and was shaved clean, and had a haircut, and some decent clothes, and although I didn't know it then, more than a hundred and fifty dollars in greenbacks in his kick. He rode a good little horse with a good saddle, and his old familiar worthless charm was almost entirely gone. He didn't offer to tell me nothing about where he'd been or what he'd been doing, and you sure don't ask in my position.

I told him if he was going into Mooney, there was a man I wanted him to be sure to look up, Madison Monroe Ambrose, who was staying on credit at the Antlers Hotel. He said he would, but it was more of a sociable answer than anything else, because he didn't ask the man's name again and looked like he was just giving me a polite answer.

He didn't get into town until noon, he dortled along so slow. He went straight to Sheriff Abe Whipple's house, and asked Edna, his wife, if Abe was to home. She said he sure was, and as companionable as a bear with a sore tail, and to go on out back and take his chances.

Abe had run out in his sock feet a couple of nights back, to pitch some rocks at some cats that was loving it up in their lilac bushes, and stepped on a piece of glass and bled like a pig. Doc Tattnal had to take four stitches to fix him up, and he told him not to set that foot on the ground for two weeks.

Abe was in an old willer chair, and Thad Rust was spading up his garden for him, and grumbling about it, and threatening to quit the county service for good. Abe didn't act like he was surprised to see Ownie, and the truth is, it took a good deal to surprise that old man. Ownie asked if he could talk to him, and Abe told Thad to get his hind end to the post office and see if there was any mail, and then go see if two drunks in the jail had sobered up enough to know their own names.

"Look at that foot!" Abe said, when Thad had went. "Felled

in my prime by a piece of glass, me that smoked out the Patterson brothers and Eben Twiss with a pretend gun! Did I ever tell you that story, Ownie?"

"Where you used a straight piece of brush for a sawed-off 10-gauge? Yes I heard it," Ownie said.

"You act like you don't believe it," Abe said.

"I believe it all right," Ownie said. "I'll believe anything after what I been through. If you've got the time, Abe, I'd like to tell you a story of my own."

"What else have I got except time, with my foot in this shape?" Abe said.

Ownie started telling him everything that had happened since they last met, how he willfully disregarded Abe's own warning to take the vengeance trail. How he met Charley Polk and they found the remains of Capistrano Erland and his horse. Abe said yes, Charley finely got around to confiding in him about that pile of human bones, although this was the first he'd had a name for them.

He told how he made out to be a mountain man, and Abe said that wasn't no play-acting, Ownie was as near to a worthless mountain man as anybody he knowed, all he had to do was not shave or cut his hair or take a bath, and he'd fool anybody. Ownie said that was just what he'd done.

He told Abe about getting a job with Blind Bosch, and keeping that a secret from them others that was jungled up out there, because no mountain man would take a job and it would of ruined his disguise. He told Abe about how the guitar drove Hart Bristol crazier than he was to begin with, and about how it was 50-50 who was going to knife who up there in the fog, until V.G. moved to adjourn by slashing into Bristol and tipping him over the edge.

He told Abe it got to be a proposition where he wasn't really looking for the other two, just killing time there on Jerry Clyde's place, and would just as soon of put off a showdown a year or two longer. Only just about the first person he run into in Denver was Jimmy Rackstraw, and you couldn't even really say the policemen killed Jimmy, he had a good chance to come out of it except for his knockers being shot off, when he ripped them bandages off.

"That just took all the heart out of me, Abe, can you understand that?" Ownie said. "You hear all the time about these people taking the vengeance trail: there was this Walcott kid in Wyoming for instance, sixteen years old when his daddy was bushwhacked by rustlers, remember?"

"Yes, I heard that story," Abe said.

"That kid stalked them rustlers for eight years before he got the last one, but he got them finely."

"Four notches on his gun finely," Abe said, "and then he come home to find his mother happily married to another man, and he killed that man too, and went outlaw, and a couple of years later was shot down in a bank holdup by the Royal Mounties."

"That's the case," Ownie said.

Abe sighed and cursed his foot some more, and said, "That's about how them stories usually end up. You hear the noble part, somebody with a brain like a rooster vows to go to the end of the earth to uphold his honor. But you don't generally hear about him flopping around in some drunken flophouse later, although that's the way it ends, because he didn't have the brains of a rooster to begin with."

Abe said, "I told you, Ownie, this was a public crime not a private feud, but you wouldn't listen, no you had to jackass yourself up in a disguise, like them knights of old, that made so much damn unnecessary trouble for everybody. It serves you right."

"I admit it," Ownie said. "I've heard of some curious vengeances in my time, but I'll be beat if this ain't the most ridiculous one on record. Jackass is right."

Abe cursed his foot some more, and said, "How about Doc Harper? Seems to me an up-and-coming gunfighter like you used to be, Doc Harper would be hard to pass up."

Ownie leaned over with his elbows on his knees and his cheeks on his fists, and stared down at the ground. "I'll see if I can line it out for you, Abe," he said, "and you tell me if you see any sense to it."

"I'll do that, never fear," Abe said.

Ownie said, "Some people can commit any kind of a crime and get away with it; they're like a doctor cutting into you, they don't think of the pain or the blood, getting the job done is all that counts, do you follow me?"

"Professionals you mean," Abe said.

"I reckon that's it," Ownie said. "Yes, that's the word I was looking for, professional; if you don't make your living at it, don't try to operate on people and don't commit no horrible felonies, because by God the odds is against you, and your own conscience is your worst enemy. Now I know you're going to say that a conscience is the last thing in the world you'd expect in people like Capistrano Erland and Hart Bristol and Jimmy Rackstraw."

"I wouldn't say anything of the kind, they're human beans same as anybody else, sons of Adam as well as sons of bitches," Abe said. "I understand what you mean, Ownie, God damn this foot of mine anyway."

"Well then," Ownie said, "you don't have to chase them people down and gun them to death, or carve them up like a mountain man, the way I was going to. You don't even have to run them down and point your finger at them and say, 'Guilty, you son of a bitch!' because in their own minds, every stranger they see is doing that; the next face they see is going to be a man that knows the truth about them and will turn them in, do you foller me?"

"Clean to the line fence," Abe said. "All you done was speed things up a little, it appears to me. Not for Capistrano, his case was closed before you assumed your damn ignorant jurisdiction, but at least Bristol and Rackstraw. What you made happen to them, it would of happened anyway sooner or later, their own guilty consciences would scream louder and louder in their own guilty ears, and they couldn't get drunk enough to drownd it out. Sooner or later it'd deadfall them."

"Right! You got the idee exactly," Ownie said. "Well then, why should I do any favors for Doc Harper? Let him live and suffer that much longer. Anyway the kind of luck I have as an avenger, some little six-year-old girl would stick her foot out just as we drawed, and he'd trip and fall with his head on a sharp rock anyway."

"Sometimes I almost have hope for you, Ownie," Abe said. "What are you going to do now?"

"I don't know yet," Ownie said. "I'm a pretty good locksmith, no don't say it, I know there's no locksmith in Mooney, but it ain't for me. I had to touch this town again somehow, kind of come a full circle; well, I've touched it and nothing is holding me. I got me some locksmith tools. Maybe I'll try Cheyenne or one of them big cities."

"Want me to tell you why?" Abe said. "Liddie."

Ownie nodded. "That's right, Liddie," he said.

"Your mother you mean?" Abe said.

Ownie said, "No, God rest her soul, I've quit fighting that devil too, I'm to blame for any thing I do, not her. I reckon my mother was no worse than some of Liddie's ancestors, or yours either for that matter. People is people, Abe, that's about how I size it up."

"I could tell you some things about my own family, say there's some corkers," Abe said. "I still don't know why you won't even go see her, though."

"Neither do I," Ownie said, "except that I know in my heart it would be a bad thing, and I ain't going to do it. For one thing, when old Liz Saymill dies, who is she going to leave all that money to?"

"Liddie prob'ly," Abe said.

"There you are," Ownie said.

Abe sighed and cursed his foot again, and said, "What are you going to do this evening? Reason I ask, Ownie, there's this big show in town, the Ambrose troupe as it's said professionally, and Edna went with some of her hen friends last night and said it's pretty good. I'd like to go if somebody would help me hobble around. I'm entitled on my badge to get us in free, so don't worry about squandering one of your precious two-bit pieces."

Ownie's idee was that a show was the last place in the world he felt like being, all he wanted to do was set under a bee tree and challenge his luck, but Abe had been pretty decent to him for a policeman, and he was a hard man to say no to at any time.

Ownie et dinner with Abe and Edna, and then him and Abe went down to the Methodist church, Abe hobbling along, leaning his weight on Ownie and cursing every step, and saying he never seen anybody clumsier than Ownie in his life, he might as well be leaning on a buffalo bull. Ownie said he was ready to turn back right now if Abe wasn't fully satisfied with the service he was getting, but they finely got there.

The lamps had already been blowed out, and Madison Monroe Ambrose was up there with one of them dazzling coal-oil reflecting spotlights on him, explaining how this funeral oration he was going to give next come about. It was just a funeral oration to the authorities, he said, but who was the authorities? Why the murderers of Caesar themselves, that was who. They had murdered Emperor Caesar and took over the government and God help anybody that took Caesar's side.

Well, he said, this fellow Marc Antony had been Caesar's friend, but he had been their friend too, Cassius and Casca and all of them, and they couldn't very well turn him down if he wanted to say a few kind words over the carcass of the diseased. "Now listen, friends," Madison Monroe Ambrose said, "and see if you don't think this is one of the most daring, as well as one of the cleverest, defiances of authority in history."

Well he really had them there, because this was a country settled by people who wouldn't of been here if they hadn't defied authority somewhere, and he dropped his voice down to a nice ringing growl, and looked down at where the coffin of Caesar would be, and then out over them people in the Methodist church like they was Romans, and began to say, "Friends, Romans, countrymen, lend me your ears, I come to *bury* Caesar, not to praise him, the evil that men do lives after them, the good is oft interred with their bones. So let it be with Caesar!"

Well this hit Ownie right where he lived, he liked nothing so much as a good successful honest double-crosser, and he was on Caesar's side to begin with, and when Ambrose said,

"So let it be with Caesar," he thought to himself why the hell with that, let's tear the town to pieces instead.

That Ambrose really had them gentled to the snaffle, there wasn't a sound in that whole churchful of people until he come to letting loose the dogs of war, and they seen it wasn't all going to blow over like they feared, and Rome was going to get a good tearing up after all. Well they just rose up and hollered, "Go to it!" and "Amen, amen," and "Give them hell there, boy," and it seemed to Ownie that this man Marc Antony must of been one of the prime sports in all of history.

Well then Ambrose had to rest while they moved the scenery around for the next act, and they went around and lit the lamps on both sides of the church, and Ownie let out this big sigh and sort of come sliding out of Rome a little at a time, you might say, and back to Mooney. He looked around him to see if there was anybody he knowed, and he got the surprise of his life suddenly, he really did.

It seemed to him that he was back on the vengeance trail somewhere, having a fit of extasy, and Liddie had come back to him. She had her black hair kind of loose on her head, but tied with a little ribbon behind, and she had on this white waist she'd made, with the high ruffly collar he liked so much on her.

Only this time she talked to him, for the first time in all his fits of extasy. She said, "Oh, Ownie, you came back, didn't you?"

Abe leaned over and said, "Why howdy there, Liddie, howdy, Liz, imagine running into you here. I reckon you remember Ownie Cope."

Liz started to sob all over the place, but she got out yes, she did seem to remember him, what a coincidence to meet, and so on. Ownie seen he'd been deadfalled worse than Cassius and Casca, God have mercy on their souls, but he didn't hardly see what he could do about it.

He said, "Yes, I come back, I don't know why except it was like I was being pulled by the bridle. I made a total complete mess of everything, but I'm back."

Liddie touched his cheek with the ends of her fingers, *she* didn't care how many people was watching, not that girl, and she said, "That's all that counts, you're back. You see prayer does help, I prayed every night you'd come to no harm, oh if you'd died, Ownie, if I'd had another grave to mourn—!"

"You knowed what I was doing?" he said.

Liz Saymill said, "You idiot, the dogs in the street knew and gossiped about it, you're as transparent as any other vain headstrong willful *thing* of a man, what do you care the evil you wreak, if your vanity is soothed? But so help me Father, Son, and Holy Ghost, you'll live up to your brief moment of holiness now, you renegade you!"

Ownie catched both sides of his head in his hands and said, "Goddlemighty, Miss Liz, you mean you'd stand for it yourself, me and her?"

"Out, out, out," she said.

Ownie got out, and Liddie got out, and the two of them went stumbling back through that church with the whole town watching, and then when he got her outside he couldn't make himself say it, he just dropped down on his knees and started kissing the ends of her fingers, until she made him stand up and do it right.

The Queen of England couldn't of done it with more style, no, nor the Empress Eugénie neither, the little girl from the wagons had them both choking on her dust. She whispered, "Whatever I am, Ownie, you saved my life, and I'm yours to the end, never forget that!" It wasn't quite that simple, a party by the name of Pete Heath had a little to do with saving her life, and so did Charley Polk and a few other people, but when she said it she believed it, and you couldn't hardly call it a lie.

They just forgot about the rest of the show, walking up and down in the dark in front of the church on that old steep brick sidewalk with tree roots sticking up through it. When Abe Whipple come hobbling out, cursing his bad foot, they was standing there looking at each other, him with his hands on her shoulders, Liddie holding onto his wrists. Just looking at each other.

"Well there you are," Abe said. "Here's somebody wants to meet you, Ownie, and then he has to go back and do up the second half of the show. Mr. Ambrose, this is Ownie Cope, Ownie, meet Mr. Madison Monroe Ambrose."

"Howdy," Ownie said, and started to turn his back, because he had more important things to do than talk to some old geezer with one foot in the grave.

"Yes, Mr. Cope, Pete Heath mentioned you. I've been so eager to meet you, I wonder if you're the son of Bessie Cope of St. Louis, I know she left a son by the name of Owen," Ambrose said.

All of the stars went out for Ownie, because he hadn't been long in the habit of forgiving his mother, and it hadn't took root very deep in him. He let go of Liddie and said, "My mother's name was Bessie, yes, what about it?"

"I knew her so well!" Ambrose said. "Your father too. You don't remember him I'm sure, he lost both legs at the knees in the war, and became a Mississippi river steamboat gambler. The most honest gambler on the river, it was universally acknowledged, and the shrewdest. Bessie and my sister were chums, ah yes indeed, I knew her that long ago!"

He said, "I wondered what became of you, Owen. Your mother's family cut her off when she married your father, as I'm sure you know. She went with him on the river boats, up and down, up and down, and took care of him until the end. He died when you were about three, you know. A gallant spirit, a fine gentleman, and he played the best poker in the history of the game."

He said, "It was the only trade your mother knew. She traveled up and down the river, up and down, up and down, playing poker as your father had taught her to play—good poker, almost as good as his! I never heard an oath in her presence, no not so much as a sharp word, Bessie Cope was a real lady in the finest sense of the word and no one failed to appreciate it."

He said, "The packet lines vied to have her aboard, she gave tone to the passage, and kept the crooks out of the games. I was in Inja when she died of typhoid, I was playing to Her Majesty's troops. I always wondered what had become of Owen and Bessie's boy. You look like both of them."

That's how he said it, Inja. He meant India. Old Ownie was reeling on his feet, but he lived up to it, he sure did. He slid his left arm around Liddie and put his right hand out and said, "It's my pleasure, Mr. Ambrose, and I want to thank you for that funeral oration, too. That was just fine, sir!"

"Oh, you liked it?" Ambrose cried. "I remember your mother liked Shakespeare, even as a little girl. So you have her tastes, do you?"

"I sure hope so," Ownie said.

CHAPTER 14

They was married about a week later, with Hoot squeezed into a new black suit for best man, and Rolf kind of uneasy during the service, because Sammie was expecting again, and insisted on coming, and he never knowed when she was going to turn white and start heaving. But she didn't, and he blundered through it somehow, and then they went off on a visit to Jerry Clyde for a honeymoon.

Liz had it in her head they was going to move in with her, and Ownie was going to start a locksmith business, and she'd start him off by having him change the locks on her house. But Ownie wanted to look this proposition in the Rockies over again, and see what Liddie thought of it, before he let Liz start running his life.

They rented a team and buggy from the livery barn to go up to the Q to catch the Denver train. They come past my place on the way, to say good-by and one thing and another, and I reckon Liddie wanted to see Pete Heath's Place again, and make sure she was grateful to God in her heart for all that had happened since she first seen it.

"You know you was who I wanted to be my best man," Ownie said. "You let me down there, Pete."

"I don't see it that way," I said. "When you launch off on something as risky as getting married, you want all the omens you can get. I wouldn't of added nothing to no wedding, believe me."

"You just ducked out of going to church is all," Ownie said. "If Rolf had shut up about it, you'd of been there."

I said well, Rolf did appear a mite too anxious, and sooner or later he'd get me, on my deathbed if not before. But I said the main reason was him and Liddie deserved a whole new deck, with the seal unbroken, and not any old shot-up spooks out of the unhappy past.

He left V.G. with me to take care of until he got back. I had to chain that dog up again, the first time he'd been on a chain since Ownie stole him from me, and then he wouldn't eat until finely I brought him in the house like he was another person. Then he ate.

They was gone until the middle of August. They moved in

with Liz Saymill, who was getting a little feeble and forgetful, and Ownie opened a locksmith shop in the Griffin Block, and repaired guns besides, and sent off for a lathe so he could even turn a barrel for you.

That was another hot August, but they all come to an end, and I remember the date clearly, the fourth of September, because I was in Mooney myself then for one of my rare infrequent visits to get a couple of horses shod. I was in Ownie's shop whiling away a hot day, and watching him file down a piece of brass to make a new part for an old grandfather's clock he was fixing, and wishing I had a good cold bottle of beer.

When Abe Whipple walked in and took off his hat and throwed it down on the counter, and said, "Ownie, guess what."

I didn't like the way he said it, and I reckon neither did Ownie, because he really jerked his head up. "He's here," he said.

"Yes he is," Abe said. "Put his horse up at the barn and arranged for a room over the barn as nervy as you please."

"And there ain't a thing you can do about it," Ownie said.

"Not a thing," Abe said. "That's what gets me, the nerve of the son of a bitch."

"What else can he do?" Ownie said.

"That's right, what else can he do?" said Abe. "But it still takes nerve."

I asked them who they was talking about, and Ownie said, "Doc Harper."

Abe said, "Yes, Doc Harper. How did you find out about it anyway, Ownie?"

"I didn't," Ownie said. "I been expecting him for quite a while, Abe."

"Why?" Abe said. "I want to hear it in your own words."

"Well," said Ownie, "what else can he do? Who could testify against him? Hart Bristol and Capistrano Erland and Jimmy Rackstraw, and they're all dead. Except for one thing, he's free as a bird, not a witness that can pin one single individual thing against him on them blowhole murders."

"You," Abe said. "Well, Ownie, there's many another man

besides you talking about this son of a bitching no-good gunfighting blowholer."

"Yes," Ownie said, "but they never claimed to be gunfighters like me. They never set out on the vengeance trail like me. They never talked to the only eye-witnesses like I talked to Hart Bristol, did they? All this other talk you're talking about, where does it come from? Me!"

He said, "Another thing, Abe, you said it yourself, this fella is a professional. He has went around the country for years and years, gunfighting for a living. He done a stretch in the pen and come right out and what did he do? Went back to gunfighting again."

He said, "Doc Harper's another kind of furry dog from them other three. He's still a blowholer, don't you ever mistake it otherwise. Somewhere in him there's still a streak of yellow. But I done plenty of thinking before I passed up that job with Jerry Clyde. That's where I'd like to be right now, out there raising cows in the mountain meadows, and bringing up a family where kids have got a chance, not here in a crowded stinking town as big as Mooney."

He said, "But it come over me that Doc Harper had to come looking for me, and when he did, by God, I better be where it meant something, where we *settled* it finely, not out there in the mountains where it would be just another gunfight. Make him come here!"

"You made him come here, all right," Abe said.

Owen took the brass out of the vice and put it away in a drawer, and slid his file nice and neat into the sheath on the wall. He smiled and said, "How does it feel to have your tail in the crack finely, Mr. Sheriff?"

Abe just cursed something awful. "I can arrest him," he said. "I can charge him with the murders. I can lock him in jail. But then what? Who can testify against him? Liddie can't. Hoot can't. Miles James can file charges against him, but it's hard enough for Miles to convict somebody with a hundred and fifty witnesses, let alone none. Andy would have to turn him loose, and why he might as well give him a signed endorsement! That's why I ain't going to arrest him, because turning him loose after that is all he needs really."

"He needs more than that," Ownie said, and he opened up the drawer under his workbench and took out his .45 wrapped up in the holster, that he hadn't wore since they come back from the honeymoon in the Rockies. "He needs more than that, a lot more," he said.

"You Goddamn fool bridegroom," Abe said. "You think you're going to outdraw Doc Harper? *Doc Harper?*"

"Like shooting fish in a barrel," Ownie said, and opened up the gun to make sure it was loaded and oiled and working.

Abe just snorted. "You ain't going out of this shop with that gun on," he said. "I won't allow it."

Ownie buckled the gun on. "There's nothing you can do about that either, Abe. Only thing you can do, you can pass the word to Harper that I ain't looking for him but I ain't running from him either. If there's going to be a killing, he has to start it."

"You mean draw first," Abe said.

"Draw first," Ownie said.

"You poor pitiful fool, so now you're going to go out there and give him first draw, and outdraw a *professional,*" Abe said.

"Yes I am," Ownie said, "and beat him, and do you know why? Because I'm a professional too. I'm working as a locksmith, because a man can be professional at more than one thing. But right now I doubt if there's a man in the world that can get a .45 out faster than me, or shoot it straighter as it comes out."

Abe looked at me like he was about ready to bust into tears, and he said, "Oh shit listen to him, now he's the best there is; how about Teddy Schmitz or Lou Kelly or Buster Gutierrez or Brazos Bill Watson, he's better than them too I guess."

Ownie said, "Lou Kelly got killed a couple of months ago in California, shotgunned down by a posse, didn't you hear about that? He wasn't much anyway, mostly blowhard. But today I could kill Teddy Schmitz and then Buster Gutierrez and then Brazos Bill Watson one at a time. I honestly could, Abe."

He said, "I'm fast enough and I shoot straight enough, and the main thing is, Abe, *I ain't afraid of nothing!* No man ever was cooler than me, why a bumblebee could light on me and I wouldn't even twitch my hide like a horse. Why should I? Do you know any man with more to live for, or be proud of, or look forward to, than me?"

"Them's going to make the handsomest last words that ever became a legend by God," Abe said. "You son of a bitch, you're bound and determined to make Liddie a widow, ain't you?"

"No, I'll kill this one," Ownie said. "I couldn't do it in cold blood to them others. But I know what you've got to be to make a gunfighter better than you do, Abe. I always was mean enough, but now I'm proud enough too."

"What about afterward, when somebody else comes after you, as they're bound to," Abe said.

"Oh hell, Abe, you take Doc Harper too serious," Ownie said. "He ain't in a class with Teddy Schmitz and Buster Gutierrez and Brazos Bill Watson. Maybe he thinks he is, but they sure don't."

Abe seen he had his mind made up. He said, "You look just as natural, Ownie! It's hard to believe you're a dead man."

Ownie said, "Oh go on, pass the word to this idiot, he's on the wrong side of the law here and so forth. I'll take all the edge I can get. Nerves is half the battle."

"I already done that," Abe said. "I hunted him up as soon as I heard. I tried to talk to him about them blowhole murders but he stood on his rights and told me to shut up or draw my gun. I had to back off on that, but I told him I wanted him out of here by sundown or I'd run him out feet first if I had to."

"What did he say to that?" Ownie said.

Abe cursed and said, "He said sundown was plenty for no more than he had to do in this farmer town. He said to tell the punkin-rollers and shuck-ears not to worry, he was soon on his way, and they could come out from under the house and slop their pigs in peace."

Ownie laughed right out loud, and said, "He honestly said

that? He had to brag did he. A wild old range rider. Well let's get it over with."

It just took your breath. He put his hat on and fitted it down over his head nice and tight, and strolled out of there into the sunshine, and stood there a minute until his eyes got used to it. That shows you that he was fairly professional at that, to think of his eyes.

He seen Bountiful Meredith across the street, carrying a forty-eight-pound sack of flour home on his shoulder, and he called out, "Howdy, Bountiful, haven't seen you since I got back, how's your missus?"

Bountiful said, "You won't see me now either, what the hell you trying to do to me, leave me out of it." He hurried on down the street, like if Ownie would of said one more word to him, he would of throwed the family flour away and run like an antelope.

"How are you betting, Pete?" Abe said.

I told him I never bet against my own horse or hand, and he said neither could he, although from all he'd heard about Doc Harper, he had a chance to make a little money off'n me. I got up and went to the window to watch, and after a minute Abe did too.

"Someday," he said, "it's going to be possible to make a man take his gun off the minute he comes to town, and an officer of the law will be an officer of the law then, not a sham and a pretense."

"But not yet," I said.

"Look at the son of a bitch," Abe said. "I only hope to God it's over before Liddie hears."

"It will be," I said, because this stranger with the broken nose come out from around the corner across the street, and pushed his hat back on his head, and a couple of boys in front of the blacksmith shop scooted inside like their tails was afire.

Up the street, Ownie was sauntering along with his back to us, just sauntering, kind of looking around on both sides like he was curious but really didn't give much of a damn. You couldn't beat it for nerve. He must of knowed him and Doc Harper was the only two men on that street, he *had* to know it, and yet he just sauntered, there's no other word for it.

"You!" Doc Harper yelled out.

Ownie turned around, about half of the block away, and said, "Who do you mean, me?"

"Yes I mean you, are you Ownie Cope?" Doc said.

"Now you know damn well I'm Ownie Cope, Ownie Cope himself, the one and only," Ownie said.

He turned around and began sauntering towards Doc, kind of grinning, and Doc said, "Then you're who I been looking for. I had to chase you halfway across the state of Colorado to catch up with you and your dirty lies; now say it to my face why don't you, let's get this settled once and for all, you lying son of a bitch."

"It's all right with me that way," Ownie said. "All I ever said about you was that Doc Harper was a dirty filthy cowardly murdering son of a bitch of a blowholer, the lowest of the low, you helped kill John Houten Swiverton and Alice Swiverton, and I talked to the men that was in with you on it. Now does that clear things up for you, you dirty murdering son of a bitch?"

It was all over then, any time a man in Doc's position lets you stand there in the street and make a campaign speech, he hasn't got blood in his veins, he's got you know what. And Doc seen it too late, he didn't have the blood he needed for this one.

"Draw!" he said. "Draw or I'll shoot you down like a dog."

"Draw yourself," Ownie said, and began walking towards him. "The last of the blowholers, that's you. You ain't got long to live you know. Either you draw, or I'll pistol-whip you to death. A little more fight in me than there was in that little girl, ain't there, you son of a bitch! Draw why don't you, draw, draw, draw!"

He wasn't no more than five or six feet away when that famous gunman Doc Harper went for his weapon, and what he looked like when he done it was some old derelict that you might find laying drunk in front of your store some morning when you went to sweep out to open up. Not that he floundered around like no farm boy in getting his gun out, no sir.

But Ownie was just pure rattlesnake, the grin went off'n his face when he went into motion, and here was this .45 in his hand before you really seen him move, and he plugged Doc twice as fast as he could pull the trigger, right in the middle of the chest. You could of put your hand over both holes.

They say a dead man falls forward on his face, and maybe he does usually, but not when he's been slapped by two .45 slugs. Doc leaned backward fast and fell hard, and Abe went sprinting out of the door bellowing for witnesses, and I reckon thirty or forty come leaking out of them buildings as fast as they could come. Anyways, I never did have to testify at the inquest, and a good thing, because I can do without a courthouse as well as I can a church.

I didn't hear the last of it by any means, though, because when Ownie and Liddie had their first baby, it was a boy, a little wrinkled ugly black-headed red-faced thing that hardly ever shut up. If he wasn't squalling about one thing, it was another.

Anyways they named him Peter Heath Cope out of a clear sky, although Pete Heath wasn't my real name and Ownie knowed it. But him and Liddie both wanted to do something for me they said, because where would they of been if I hadn't brought Hoot in out of the storm, and then harnessed up my own four-horse team the next morning. What really gave me a turn was that old Liz Saymill said she thought I was entitled, and it was an attractive name besides, and maybe some of her critics was right when they said the old girl was getting childish in her old age.

I had to go to the son of a bitching babtism and christening, and stand godfather to this ugly little squalling papoose, and hold him while Rolf wet him down as he said the words, not that he needed wetting. He was the pissingest baby you ever seen, Ownie admitted that himself, he said he was just like a funnel, in at one end and out the other.

I got through it all right, you ain't going to throw me by making an exhibition of me, because I've got my own kind of stubborn vain bullheaded pride. I always figger if I'm forced to go somewhere, and I'm out of place there, the hell with it, let others get up and leave if they don't like it.

We got the job done, and Ownie and Liddie loped off with their kid, Peter Heath Cope, because it was fixing to rain and God knew that kid was already soaked from enough causes. Rolf said, "Thanks a lot, Pete, for taking on this chore. I know you hate it, but it meant a lot to Ownie and Liddie, and Hoot too for that matter."

"I notice Hoot ducked it," I said.

"He didn't duck it," he said. "He busted an ankle yesterday, his horse quit on him and let a steer drag it. It's Hoot's own fault, only a three-year-old colt, but you know these smart-aleck kids, they got to prove the colt they broke is as steady as your weary old veteran cow horse."

"That's only the start," I said. "Wait till he's my age, and all stove up and scarred and twisted, he won't think so much of being a cowboy."

Rolf said, "You never worked at cowboying long enough to get saddle sores even! But life has been good to both of us in spite of our natural orneriness, Pete. And look at Ownie and Liddie, and think back to what life had to offer them both, that morning of the blizzard! Ain't you about ready to admit that the good Lord is entitled to some thanks for what He done for all of us, and come be a member of the church where you're always welcome?"

I said, "Well, Rolf, I ain't ready to go that far yet. But I do have to admit, lately it looks like He's got a kind of a streak going for Him."